·"Wh

Humili... ...s
of passersby. "I didn't do nothin'—"

"So *you* say," the policeman returned, not slowing one
whit. "The *gentleman* says—"

"He's no gentleman—"

"The gentleman says you were trying to steal his wallet."

"I wasn't. That's not the way it was at all. When I wouldn't
go with him, he grabbed me."

"Now, missy, I ask you." The beefy-faced man gave her
an insulting smile. "Who would you believe if you was me?
An ignorant guttersnipe, or a gentleman—a *gentleman*," he
repeated,"with a bloody nose."

"He deserved it!" Even as she trembled with trepidation,
Mary's eyes held righteous indignation. "And if he's a gentleman, I'm the Queen of England."

DIANNA CRAWFORD AND RACHEL DRUTEN

Dianna

are California natives who joined their talents to tell a beautiful story. They also work together in a program of tutoring, art, and music called "TAM." The purpose of the program is to offer at-risk children mentors for the present, a vision for the future, and the tools to achieve their vision.

Dianna has been published since the early 1990s and writes full-time. Her first inspirational novel was the premier of a six-book series for Tyndale that she coauthored with Sally Laity. Dianna is married and has four daughters and seven grandkids.

When not writing, Rachel is an artist who paints portraits. Her family includes a husband and two grown children. *Out of the Darkness* is Rachel's first published inspirational romance.

Rachel

Don't miss out on any of our super romances. Write to us at the following address for information on our newest releases and club information.

Heartsong Presents Readers' Service
PO Box 719
Uhrichsville, OH 44683

Out
of the Darkness

Dianna Crawford
Rachel Druten

Heartsong Presents

Dedicated to the memory of Daniel Bryant and his wife, Emma. Their mission in South Africa is still alive today.

Acknowledgment: For their generous help and encouragement we thank Mary Firmin, Sheila Herron, Jeri Levy, Sue Rich, Barbara Wilder, and husband, Charles Druten. And finally, to Daniel and Emma's great-grandson, Daniel Bryant, who came to know them through the letters he found in the old green trunk that made this book possible.

A note from the authors:
We love to hear from our readers! You may correspond with us by writing: **Dianna Crawford and Rachel Druten**
Author Relations
PO Box 719
Uhrichsville, OH 44683

ISBN 1-57748-487-8

OUT OF THE DARKNESS

All Scripture quotations are from the Authorized King James Version of the Bible unless otherwise noted.

Except for references to the Bryants all of the characters and events in this book are fictitious. Any resemblance to actual persons, living or dead, or to actual events is purely coincidental.

Cover illustration by Jocelyn Bouchard.

PRINTED IN THE U.S.A.

one

Johannesburg, South Africa
January 1905

Colin Reed felt his friend's hand on his shoulder.

"What are you grinning at?" Henry asked.

"A woman."

"That good, huh?" Henry Harcourt leaned forward, squinting out the third-story window as if he, too, could see what Colin spied through the telescope.

Colin's smile broadened. He glanced up at his always enthusiastic, ever curious chum who'd aimed his new telescope, not toward the *stars*, but two miles away at the main street of the booming gold rush town. "Actually, I was wondering what your charming wife would say if I brought someone like that to one of her tea parties."

"Let me see." Henry nudged Colin aside and put an eye against the finder. Hunched over his latest toy, Henry's pudgy fingers eagerly twisted the knobs, as if finding the woman were some new and exciting game.

Colin marveled at the short, stout man. It seemed Henry had changed hardly a whit since they roomed together at Oxford University. Even with a wife and two small children, he lived life with the same carefree exuberance. . .a trait that still engaged the more intellectual and competitive Colin. Henry was always good for a laugh—a much-needed tonic now that Colin had been appointed district magistrate to this northern province.

His chest tightened at the thought. Sometimes he wondered if he'd bitten off more than he could chew in this job. Ever since the civil war, there had been such bitterness between the Dutch Boers and the English that maintaining order up here was next to impossible.

He shifted his gaze to the windows along the west wall of Henry's third-floor sanctuary. Why couldn't the tranquillity of the rolling hills of the veldt spill over into the rest of Transvaal on this balmy summer's day?

To make matters worse, he had to deal with the riffraff pouring into Johannesburg from every corner of the world. He pictured the gold fields to the northeast, men crawling over the mutilated land like maggots devouring a decaying carcass, every one of them determined to strike it rich by hook or by crook.

More often by crook, judging from his overcrowded jail.

Henry laughed. "I see your woman! You're right, ol' chap. Sylvia would have both our hides if you brought that kind of lady to tea. She's got more plumage than a peach-faced lovebird."

"Plumage?" Colin turned back to Henry. "I'd hardly call a gray shirtwaist and skirt plumage. Who are *you* looking at?"

The shorter man stepped aside and Colin eased his own eye down again to the finder, careful not to move the scope. Even from this distance he could clearly see one of Fourth Street Ryzzi's brassy-haired women languishing in a doorway while a couple of men haggled over her—none of them in the least concerned that the district courthouse—*his* courthouse—was just three doors down. "That's not the woman."

"Then find me someone else out there worth looking at."

Colin moved the scope, hoping to catch another glimpse of the little gray wren who'd caught his eye. "Ah, there she is." He watched her angle across the wide street, weaving between the wagons and street vendors' carts and a various assortment of ne'er-do-wells loitering in front of the farmers market exchanging bottles—and outrageous lies.

In her path, blacks and coloreds meandered with serpentine grace through the clusters of Europeans, their dusky skin gray with the street's dust. He saw her give a wide berth to a man lounging in front of the barber shop.

Colin flinched, recognizing the fellow as one he suspected of procuring girls from Russia and New York to service the miners.

And through this milieu marched that small, simply dressed woman. She carried herself stiff as a sergeant-major, her modest bonnet squarely on her head, determination in every stride. There was such honesty in every move. . .and something else. A vulnerability. Perhaps it was the way she clutched her little purse to her breast.

But what was she doing down there alone? Any decent woman would know she shouldn't be on the streets of Johannesburg unescorted.

Yet there she was, so resolute, so focused. . .too focused. "For heaven's sake, woman, get out of the middle of the street," Colin said aloud. "That wagon missed her by a whisper."

"My peach-faced lovebird?" Henry asked, hovering at Colin's shoulder.

"No. My little gray wren."

"Let me see this wren of yours." As soon as Colin stepped back, Henry moved in to take over again. "That *plain* one? She'll surely be no competition to the other ladies on the block," he snorted. "Really, Colin, your taste has certainly deteriorated since our college days. Here, Sylvia has been introducing you to the cream of genteel society, the prettiest young things for miles around—and you're interested in *her?*" Henry shook his head.

In truth, Colin was interested. Maybe because she *didn't* look like she belonged "on the block," as Henry put it. Either block. And maybe because there was something familiar about her that intrigued him. But he wasn't about to admit that to Henry. "I didn't say I was interested."

"Well, that's a relief, because Sylvia's invited a beauty to tea that you won't be able to resist."

"Ah, no. Not again." A weariness settled over Colin. He raked a hand through his unruly black curls. "You said it would just be the three of us this time."

"So I did." Remorse stamped Henry's freckled face. "It was supposed to be. But then Sylvia's friend from England suddenly arrived with her father. And well, you know Sylvia, she wanted to be the first to entertain her. Trust me, old man, this time you won't be disappointed." He put his eye again to the scope. "She's absolutely stunning, and a British aristocrat to boot. Certainly not some common little street sparrow."

Colin groaned. The gold strike had made Henry's banking family as rich as Eastern potentates. His gaze scanned his friend's ballroom-size hideaway cluttered with eccentric inventions and expensive gadgets. Yet no amount of Henry's money could purchase what Sylvia coveted most—a place in England's upper class. Ever since she'd returned home to South Africa after the Boer War, the elegant order of that faraway life was all she'd striven to recreate.

And, more irritating, all she ever talked about.

Which was precisely what Colin had been trying to avoid ever since his forthright mother died and his father had married an older, more accomplished, more sweetly manipulative version of Sylvia.

In these days of a newly united and grandly prosperous South Africa, would nothing more substantive be produced in the way of marriageable maidens than a useless English lady? If that were so, Colin just might become what Sylvia was already calling him—a confirmed bachelor.

He grimaced. Maybe he'd be better off just chucking it all and becoming a professional hunter—live his life in the wilds.

"Why that villain," Henry murmured. "He just absconded

with two live chickens." He looked up at Colin. "This is a good vantage point for surveillance, old friend. You might just have to deputize me."

"You'd like that," Colin muttered, taking the toy for himself.

He scanned the street, but didn't find the thief. And where had his little gray wren gone? Then he found her, striding toward the dry goods store. She looked over her shoulder as a man in an expensively tailored suit approached her. *Uh-oh.* Colin knew him from the Athletic Club, the solicitor who usually had had one too many.

The man tipped his bowler.

Now she's in for it. I wouldn't trust my grandmother within a mile of that lecher.

If the set of her chin was any indication, the girl shared his opinion. . . Ha! She was giving him an earful—feisty little thing. "The scoundrel!" Colin exploded. "He just grabbed her."

"Who?"

"The girl."

"Let me see." Henry tried to regain the telescope, but Colin wasn't about to relinquish it this time.

The young woman's gray bonnet sailed through the air, releasing a cascade of auburn curls that blew across her face. She was holding her ground, fighting the man off. She drew back. With all her might, she smacked the lout across his mouth with her purse. Out of her hands it flew, the contents scattering in all directions.

"Why won't someone help her? My men. *Where are my men?*"

Colin's outrage fueled his sense of duty. He thrust aside the telescope and purposefully rose to his full six-feet-three inches. "I have to go."

"Don't be ridiculous." Henry had assumed the telescope again. "She's two miles away. By the time you arrive it will all be over—atta girl. She just kicked him in the shin."

"Let me see." Colin tried to grab the instrument, but Henry wasn't budging.

"Ah, at last." Henry began a running discourse as Colin paced. "Johannesburg's finest has just arrived. Constable Peterson, all decked out in his starched best, brandishing his faithful nightstick."

"It's about time." With some force Colin pushed his friend aside.

"So you like my new toy," Henry murmured.

Colin didn't bother to placate him; his attention was riveted on the scene two miles away. "That dunderhead, Peterson. He's arrested the wrong person. He's taken the *girl* into custody." Colin wheeled away and strode to the double doors. "I must go back to town and straighten this out."

"Straighten what out?" Henry caught up, grabbing Colin's arm. "You don't know what's been said down there. There's probably a lot more to it. Besides, you can't go now." His voice rose in panic. "Sylvia will kill me—"

"I have to, Henry. It's my duty."

Henry was at Colin's heels as he headed down the stairs. "You know Sylvia's going to blame me for this. She'll murder me, and then you'll *really* have your hands full."

"Tell her I'll return within the hour. Explain the urgency. She'll understand."

"What? That you left her party to go chasing after some floozy? I doubt that."

Colin took the steps two at a time down the sweeping spiral staircase. He crossed the ebony-floored foyer, dodging the marble-maiden fountain and the potted palm. He'd just reached the front door as the bell clanged. Without waiting for the servant, he pulled it open.

He came face to face with an elegant young lady, her afternoon gown such a gossamer shade of green, it looked to have been spun of the sea. From beneath the brim of a flower-bedecked bonnet, an incredible pair of sapphire eyes smiled up into his.

Colin paused, then breathed in the scent of lilacs that wafted on the halo of sunlight surrounding this vision.

two

Mary's heart pounded. "I didn't do nothin'," she railed, struggling to break the viselike grip on her arm. But the ape of a man in the khaki uniform paid her no heed as he dragged her, the innocent victim, up the steps of the Johannesburg police station.

Even back home, in a city huge as New York, nothing like this had ever happened to her. Officer Chancy had been more than just a policeman on the block, he'd been her friend, her protector.

"Why don't you believe me?" Humiliation coursed through her as she felt the curious glances of passersby. "I didn't do nothin'—"

"So *you* say," the policeman returned, not slowing one whit. "The *gentleman* says—"

"He's no gentleman—"

"The gentleman says you were trying to steal his wallet."

"I wasn't. That's not the way it was at all. When I wouldn't go with him, he grabbed me."

"Now, missy, I ask you." The beefy-faced man gave her an insulting smile. "Who would you believe if you was me? An ignorant guttersnipe, or a gentleman—a *gentleman*," he repeated, "with a bloody nose."

"He deserved it!" Even as she trembled with trepidation, Mary's eyes held righteous indignation. "And if he's a gentleman, I'm the Queen of England."

"The Queen of England doesn't filch wallets." The officer pushed her through the open doorway. "You foreigners may think anything goes, but filching a gentleman's wallet is just as much against the law here as anywhere else. At least as long as Constable Peterson's on the job."

"Why won't you believe me?" The more she struggled, the tighter her captor's grip became. Suddenly, fury at the injustice of it swept away her fear. And her good sense. "Unhand me you—you. . .oaf!!" she sputtered, grappling with renewed vigor.

"Just calm down, missy." The constable squeezed her arm until she winced. "It's not going to help your case to resist arrest. I'll just have to add it to my report." His unctuous tone echoed through the central hall as he shoved her into an office on their left.

The fair-sized room held six desks, three on either side, facing front. At the struggling pair's noisy entrance, an officer glanced up briefly, then returned to the newspaper he was reading.

No help from that quarter.

Mary took a deep breath. *You've been through bad scrapes before, lass. New York with your dad was no stroll in the park. You survived him. You can survive anything.*

And she had. With a drunken lout of a father, the responsibility for two younger brothers had fallen to her when their mother died of influenza. Her life had consisted of working at the factory from dawn to dusk, six days a week, then rushing home to get food on the table.

No, indeed, life had been no bed of clover. She'd just have to look at this as another hurdle to overcome.

She'd handle it—and everything else the day had wrought. She had no choice.

Mary drew herself up to her full five feet three inches and, with a bravado she was far from feeling, looked sternly into her captor's eyes. "I'll thank you to unhand me, sir."

"Well, ain't we the hoity-toity one, all of a sudden." A taunting smile played beneath the constable's mustache as he looked down over his considerable girth. But finally, he did release her and, with mock courtesy, ushered her to a chair angled before a desk in the rear.

Mary sat, her back stiff, her hands clutched tightly in her lap.

Removing his cap, Constable Peterson lowered himself behind a scarred desk. His bulk filled the chair as he rocked back, assessing her through pale, narrowed eyes.

She tightened her lips to keep them from trembling and met his scrutiny with an unflinching gaze. "I'd be obliged if you'd return what belongs to me. Namely, my purse." She looked down. It lay on the desk where the constable had dropped it, a drawstring pouch that appeared more like a dead bird, lying between them, gray and lifeless.

He covered it with a beefy hand. "It'll be safe with me, missy," he informed her as he pulled a form and pen from the middle desk drawer. Elaborately, he dipped the tip into an inkwell and poised it above the sheet before him. "Name?"

"I done nothin' wrong." Her voice rang louder than she'd intended, and the officer at the middle desk glanced up. Constable Peterson rolled his eyes and shrugged. Clearly, her name was of little consequence. He wouldn't believe her anyway.

Beneath her bravado, Mary's heart sank.

"Address?"

"So you can go and paw through my belongin's like you did my purse?" She leaned forward. "You can't do this to me. I have my rights. I'm an American citizen."

"So you are, missy, so you are." A cold, cunning smile pierced the officer's eyes. "And no doubt one of Ryzzi Kryzika's loveliest. Brought all the way from New York to entertain the miners."

Horrified, Mary drew herself upright. "I ain't no such thing. I may have been on the same ship as him, but I ain't one of his girls, that's for sure. He's my husband's. . .acquaintance. Just an acquaintance. Nothin' more than that!"

"You have a husband?" The constable's bushy eyebrows lifted.

Mary nodded, hope springing into her heart.

"Why didn't you say so?"

"You didn't give me no chance," she answered, emboldened by his reaction.

"What kind of husband would allow a decent woman to go out alone on the streets of Johannesburg?" His eyes narrowed once more. "You sure your husband's connection to Fourth Street Ryzzi isn't business?"

Mary's heart faltered, but righteous indignation lifted her chin again. "How dare you—"

"Very well. Where can we find him?"

"His name's Ed McKenzie. But—" Mary's voice lost power. "I don't know where he's at."

"Uh-huh." Not even bothering to look at her, the man sent a line through something on the form. Everything about him bespoke his disbelief.

"He heard about a new strike in the north. . .yesterday." It sounded false even to her.

"Inconvenient for you," Constable Peterson murmured, filling out more spaces on the page.

Oh, how Mary wished she could read so she'd know what he was writing.

"Ed left a note." A note she'd had to rely on the desk clerk to read to her. "It said Mr. Kryzika had offered to look after me. Ed didn't know he was a vile peddler of flesh. He wouldn't have left me here if he had." She heard her voice rise again in desperation.

"*Ladies* don't walk the streets in this part of town. Even ignorant foreigners know that," the officer snorted.

"I was just out lookin' for some honest work."

"Certainly your *husband* left you some money?"

Mary hung her head. "Only what's in my purse."

The constable reached inside the sad little pouch. "This?" He held up her two one-pound notes. "This is all you have?"

"That's why I was lookin' for work."

"Now *that* I believe." Constable Peterson laid down his pen and leaned back. He put his elbows on the arms of the chair and steepling his fingers over his belly, scrutinized her with skeptical eyes. "The question is, just what kind of work were you seeking?"

"I'm a very good seamstress. I was the fastest girl in the factory attachin' sleeves."

The man laughed. "Only the sleeves? I doubt there'll be much call for sleeve attachers here." He sat forward and added a final postscript to the form, then pushed it toward Mary and handed her the pen. "Sign at the bottom of the page."

She tried to make out some words. She was sure "guilty" started with a *g*. But there were so many words, and the constable kept glowering at her. "What if I don't want to?"

"You don't know how to write."

"Of course I do." She grabbed the paper, and to prove it, she signed her name—carefully, as her younger brother Brody had taught her.

Constable Peterson rose and put on his cap. "Now missy, we'll just keep you safe until the magistrate gets here to set your bail."

Mary could hardly breathe. "You're still gonna arrest me? After what I told you?"

"You signed the form. You read it. . .you said."

Dumbly, she followed him along a hall lined with offices. A woman brushed past, a man called to someone through an open door. But she was only vaguely aware of the surroundings as her captor herded her down a flight of stairs.

From the warren of cells in the bowels of the building, a clamor of curses and banging greeted their arrival. Crazed eyes glittered through the slits of metal doors.

Assaulted by the reek of human filth and despair, Mary shrank back, as if the bulk of her jailer offered protection.

But the constable pushed her forward as she shivered in the chill of her fear.

&

Colin felt the pressure of Miss Fitzsimmon's hand in the crook of his arm. Ever so gently, she leaned against him for support as they stepped out onto the verandah.

"Please call me Grace Ellen." Her voice was light and lilting, most pleasant to his ear.

"Only if you call me Colin."

Returning a shy smile, she said, "I like the name Colin. It's such a strong name. It makes me think of knights in the olden days battling for a lady's honor."

He sensed his color rise and a not altogether unpleasant confusion.

Prettily, she slid into the chair he pulled out for her at the elegantly appointed tea table, and with a honeyed "thank you" and a flutter of incredibly long lashes, she turned her attention to the adjacent landscape. "You are a genius with flowers, Sylvia," she declared, lifting delicate lace-covered fingers in a gesture of delight. "Your garden is a veritable fairyland. The roses entwining the columns—"

"Thank you, dear." Sylvia settled into the chair opposite. "We brought P. Allen Smith down from England to design it."

"The famous horticulturist?"

Sylvia nodded, clearly pleased that her guest had recognized the name. "Sit here, Colin." She patted the seat of the peacock wicker chair between her and Grace Ellen.

"Truly spectacular," Grace Ellen said, speaking to Sylvia, but smiling at Colin.

Henry, reclining on a chaise nearby, fanned himself with a magazine as the native servant, in a black maid's uniform and frilly white cap and apron, poured spring water into fluted goblets.

Colin noticed the intricately carved jardinieres overflowing with vining pink geraniums at intervals along the polished mahogany planks, and beneath the steps, star jasmine sprawled, its fragrance heavy in the afternoon heat.

But nothing was sweeter than the subtle scent of lilacs wafting from the young woman beside him. Her perfume seemed as much her essence as the scent of a rose was to its bloom.

"Where're you staying in Johannesburg, Miss Fitzsimmon— Grace Ellen?" he asked.

"We're visiting the cousin of friends. The Norwoods. Do you know them?"

Henry helped himself to three cucumber sandwiches and a scone from the tray the servant was passing. "George belongs to our club."

And George's wife was one of Sylvia's coconspirators, Colin knew, pleased with their matchmaking choice for a change.

Grace Ellen continued, "We were thinking of renting a little house. But the Norwoods wouldn't hear of it." Her smile was coy as she held Colin's gaze.

"How long will you be staying?" he asked.

"We aren't quite sure." After a lingering moment she sighed deeply and lifted a languid hand to her breast as her eyes drifted again to the garden. "Yes, indeed, Sylvia, this spot is heaven on earth."

No expense had been spared to make it so.

Colin followed Grace Ellen's gaze over the vista of emerald lawn, where paths meandered through a grove of mulberry and liquidambar trees toward the grape arbor and an ornate gazebo. Beyond stood a statue of Venus, discreet behind a Canary Island pine.

"I found this tea service in that little antique shop you

recommended in Kensington Square," Sylvia said, tipping a delicate teapot over a matching cup. "Grace Ellen was so kind when the children and I were in London."

"Oh, so your home is in London?" Colin asked Grace Ellen.

"Well, not exactly." Through lowered lashes, she studied the contents of her cup. "Since Papa. . .retired, we've done a lot of traveling." She looked up. "He's writing a book, you know, so we go where his research leads him."

"What is his subject?" Colin asked.

"Well, he hasn't quite decided. So many fascinate him."

"She and her father stayed with the Barkleys the months they were in London," Henry offered, heaping his scone with strawberry jam. "You remember Ewing Barkley. He was in Lambert House when we were at Oxford, and from what Grace Ellen's father says, he's amassed an excellent library."

"It seems we have many friends in common, Colin," Grace Ellen said.

He smiled. "So it seems." First, the Barkleys. Now, the Norwoods. Perhaps he'd best not give his own address unless he wanted to become the next to entertain them.

The silver tongs in Sylvia's hand hovered over the sugar bowl.

"Three lumps, please—and cream," Grace Ellen said.

"You're so lucky. Every lump shows on me," Sylvia sighed, handing Grace Ellen an embroidered linen napkin beneath an embossed silver spoon.

"Charming sterling." Her guest delicately weighed the flatware between her thumb and index finger.

For a moment Colin thought she might turn it over to see the hallmark, but she didn't need to.

"George IV Fiddle pattern," Grace Ellen observed, her tone admiring.

Obviously pleased, Sylvia smiled. "You recognize it."

And the price, Colin reckoned, with the discernment gained from his profession. Lovely as she seemed, he was beginning to suspect that Grace Ellen Fitzsimmon might be a woman of calculating charm—one who made it her business to be an agreeable guest. Was it possible that her winsome ways disguised a lack of sincerity?

He hoped not. She was such a fine figure of a woman.

As she flirted with him beneath the brim of her courtier bonnet, he suddenly remembered the styleless gray hat flying from the curls of that valiant little woman on the street and felt ashamed. As incompetent as Peterson could be, at least he had *thought* he was doing his duty. Colin knew he was shirking his own. He felt an urgency to get back to the station.

"Colin! Are you with us?" Sylvia's incisive tone penetrated his thoughts. "As I was saying," she paused and fixed him with a stern gaze, "I felt so guilty in London. Here I was, being lavishly entertained in some of the finest homes in Britain while my husband and Colin were risking life and limb, battling the Boers."

Stirring her tea, Grace Ellen looked first at Henry, then at Colin. "I sensed at once I was in the presence of two heroes," she teased.

"That's—well, that's very kind of you, Grace Ellen," Henry blustered. "But I wouldn't go so far as to say that."

Colin grimaced. Indeed, if he were a true hero he would have had the courage to challenge Sylvia's disapproval and leave. He heard the clock in the parlor chime the quarter hour. Twenty minutes had elapsed since he'd seen the altercation on the street.

Sylvia handed him a cup of tea. "I know you take yours plain, Colin. Although in my opinion you could use a bit of sweetening on occasion."

Grace Ellen swept her lush-lashed gaze from Colin to her

hostess. "How can you say that, Sylvia? I find the gentleman utterly charming."

Taking a deep breath, Colin reached for an egg and olive canapé.

"Sylvia has been absolutely grand." Grace Ellen nibbled her watercress sandwich. "She's really taken us under her wing—Papa and me—introduced us to just everyone."

"And, of course, my pet saved the best for last." Henry gave a hearty laugh and handed his cup to the servant to refill.

"*Are* you the best, Colin Reed?" Grace Ellen bestowed another coy smile.

"I suppose that depends on who you ask. If my mother were alive she'd probably agree, but there are plenty of others who. . ." He shrugged.

"Oh, Colin, don't be so modest." Sylvia turned to Grace Ellen. "He wouldn't tell you this, but he's from one of the older British families of Cape Town. His father is a most respected judge. And the dear boy, himself, was recently appointed magistrate to Transvaal." She smiled at Colin. "Even the men who work for you think you're wonderful. You know they do, Colin."

"On the other hand," Henry interrupted, "if you were to poll the scoundrels he's incarcerated—"

"Speaking of which," Colin interrupted as he stood up, "I really have to go. As enjoyable as this is, there's a matter at the station that requires my immediate attention."

"You're not leaving so soon?" Sylvia sprang to her feet. "You haven't finished your tea. I wanted you to hear Grace Ellen sing. She has a lovely soprano voice that I thought would be such an addition to our musicales at the Bryants'."

"Bryants? Are they related to the Lawford-Bryants of Knightsbridge?" Grace Ellen asked, obviously doing her own best to keep Colin from leaving.

"No, these Bryants are from America."

"They're missionaries," Henry said.

"Oh. . .I see." Grace Ellen's nostrils flared delicately, as if she had just inhaled a slightly unpleasant odor.

"But lovely, elegant people." Sylvia quickly assured her. "And don't worry, dear, they won't proselytize you. Their work is mainly with the natives."

Schooling his tongue to words of polite flattery, Colin bowed slightly in Grace Ellen's direction. "I can think of nothing I'd rather do than while away a summer afternoon, listening to this lovely lady sing. But, alas, duty calls."

"Oh, Colin, I'm so disappointed," Sylvia pouted, and then her face brightened. "We'll bring Grace Ellen to the Bryants' next week." She turned to her. "Do say you'll come, dear. Emma and Daniel will love you."

When Grace Ellen's eyes lifted for Colin's confirmation, all he could manage was a noncommittal smile. "I'm sure you would be welcome." What else could he say? And of course the Bryants would welcome her. That's the kind of people they were.

"Well, I must be off. Sylvia." He kissed her hand. Then turning to Grace Ellen, "Though much too brief, it has been delightful."

With her head tilting up beneath the brim of her flowered bonnet, Grace Ellen's amazing eyes met his.

Colin had to admit, the woman was mesmerizing. She was the mistress of the slow move, the beguiling smile, the side-long glance. And she used them all.

"Will I see you soon?" she asked.

"Most assuredly." He caught the triumphant look Sylvia tossed her husband. "Next week at the Bryants'."

His host began to rise.

"I'll see myself out," Colin said. "You stay and entertain the ladies." He could hardly wait to be gone.

But as he rounded the corner of the house, up the drive trotted a brown pony pulling a bright yellow cart, carved and painted with flowers. Harry and Edlyn, the two young Harcourt children, six and four respectively, bounced within it, while their nanny strode alongside.

"Uncle Colin," the boy shrieked, reining in the pony. He leaped from the cart, the little girl tumbling after him.

"Uncle Colin, Uncle Colin," they chorused, racing toward him. They hurtled into his arms.

"Come see our new cart," Edlyn cried.

Colin glanced toward Johannesburg and sighed. The problem could wait a minute more. With such an exuberant greeting he had not the heart to disappoint the little imps.

What else could a godfather do?

&

Relative quiet cloaked the cell block. Only a disgruntled mumble, a desolate moan.

The clang of metal on metal as the cell door slammed, the clank of a bolt thrown, seemed to reverberate long after the constable's retreating footsteps faded.

Stumbling forward, Mary dropped down onto the bottom mattress of the three-tiered bunk. She pushed back the tangled hair that fell across her cheek and tried not to cry as her dulled eyes assessed the surroundings.

Lit only by a slash of light squeezing through a narrow barred window inches from the ceiling, the chamber was hardly larger than the lavatory down the hall from her family's New York tenement.

And it smelled as rank.

Retching, Mary covered her mouth with a trembling hand.

In the corner a metal-lined hole in the floor left no doubt as to the source of the fetid stench—or its rude purpose.

She buried her head in her hands. What was to become of her? No one believed her. They didn't even believe she was married. And why should they? She had nothing to prove it, not even a ring. What little money Ed had left her wouldn't even be enough to cover their hotel bill.

Had it been only this morning that she had awakened to the empty place on the bed beside her and discovered Ed's letter—and the two one-pound notes he'd left beside it? And then to find out he'd left her the bill as well. . .

How could he?

What did he expect her to do—a woman alone, an ocean away from home? She'd trusted him, believed him when he'd filled her ears with promises and dreams.

And oh, the humiliation when she'd had to ask the desk clerk to read his letter to her. How she'd suffered the skepticism in the man's voice and the nasty, knowing look when he'd read, "Don't worry, sweetheart, Ryzard Kryzika has promised to watch out for you until I come back."

Ryzard Kryzika.

Could Ed possibly have been that blind? Even she, an ignorant, illiterate girl, had seen through Mr. Kryzika, although she hadn't known then the extent of his evil.

The light was dimming with the hour and soon it would be dark. She felt the walls closing in on her and pressed her hand again to her lips. She must hold on. She must not lose control.

Oh, Ed, how could you do this to me? How could you leave me like this?

She realized, suddenly, how little she really knew of the man she had married on board ship. Ed McKenzie, her foreman at the factory where she did piecework. Ed McKenzie, who'd handed her sweet talk with the cut fabric she was to sew. This man, who in that darkest hour had been there for her—or so she'd thought.

If only they'd gone to Alaska as he'd first planned, she wouldn't be in this mess. But when they'd met Ryzzi Kryzika on the docks, and he'd told them the ship to South Africa sailed sooner, they were off, influenced by a man they barely knew.

As if a few hours should make the least difference in such a serious decision.

She wrung her hands.

Was God punishing her for what had happened to her father? For helping her brothers to escape?

Bad as it had been at home, it was nothing compared to this. In the worst of times, when her father was falling-down drunk, out of control, she had never felt so hopeless. . .or helpless. Even then, fear had not gripped her as it gripped her now.

She wrapped her arms around herself, rocking back and forth in a paroxysm of misery, remembering her brothers, Brody and Ethan, with guilt and longing. She'd been a mother to them since their own had died, protecting them from their father's unpredictable wrath. She'd been the one, not her father, who'd seen that they had clothes on their backs and food in their tummies and insisted they study and learn so they could make a better life for themselves than she'd ever be able to give them.

She loved them so. Missed them. Her heart ached with the knowledge that she'd likely never see them again, and the sadness of having to let them go West without her. Sixteen and fourteen, far too young to be on their own. But her savings weren't enough for the three of them.

She fought back the tears that sprang into her eyes, knowing if she allowed them to start, a flood would follow.

But at least the boys had each other. She had no one.

No one except that vile Ryzzi Kryzika—which was worse than no one at all. And the desk clerk. But he was hardly likely to vouch for her once he learned she couldn't pay her bill.

If only she knew where Ed was. Her only hope depended upon his return, and only God knew when that would be.

If ever.

If there was a God.

Mary became aware that the noise in the jail had sharpened—the cacophony of expletives, the pounding, clanking metal.

Maddened beasts rattling their cages.

Was she to become one of them?

She heard voices outside her cell. The scrape of the bolt being thrown. With a grating whine, the door swung open.

In the waning light, Mary recognized the bulk of Constable Peterson. "You have a visitor. . .*Mrs*. McKenzie."

Mary leaped to her feet. *Ed. Ed was back*. Her prayer had been answered.

The constable stepped aside, then slammed the cell door shut behind. . .Ryzzi Kryzika.

three

Mary's hope plummeted to despair. She swung away, unable to bear the sight of Ryzzi Kryzika's ferret eyes and twisted smile. "I suppose you're here to gloat."

"On the contrary." The little man stepped close. His hot breath singed the back of her neck. "I've come to save you."

"Save me!" Mary spun around. "It's knowin' you that's put me here. The man what grabbed me in the street thought I was one of yer girls." She glared at the flashily dressed little man who was hardly taller than she. "I wonder where he got *that* idea?"

Ryzzi Kryzika cocked his hip and shoved bony hands into the pockets of his purple pinstripe suit. "It's not so bad bein' one a my girls, ya know. I take good care a my girls—and, like I promised my good friend Ed—I–I'm willin' to take care a you. I'm here to post your bail."

"No, thank you." She turned away in disgust. "And as for bein' Ed's good friend, he hardly knew ya. If he had, he wouldn't a been so foolish as to leave me in yer filthy hands."

The man grabbed her arm. His pale eyes narrowed with a false smile. "Don't get smart with me, girly," he warned in a silky voice, "or I'll leave ya here to rot."

"I'd rather rot than be beholden to the likes o' you." Mary yanked free and pushed him aside. "Constable!" She pounded on the door of her cell. "Constable, me and Mr. Kryzika have finished our business."

But before she knew what happened, the reprobate had slammed her against the brick wall and pinned back her arms. "Don't mess with Fourth Street Ryzzi," he snarled, his face so close his features were blurred. "You got that?" His breath was as rank as the hole in the corner of the cell. Mary turned her head. He grabbed her chin and twisted her face back to his. "You got that?" Though small, he was sinewy and strong. The more she struggled, the tighter his grasp.

"Constable!" Her cry was muffled by the bruising crush of his hand over her mouth.

"Keep at it, girly. I like 'em feisty. They bring a higher price."

A higher price? Stark terror tore at Mary. Excited shouts from other cells matched her own as the evil little man pressed his body against hers, his cheek to hers, forcing her to hear his whispered threats. "If ya wanna see your sweet Eddie again, you'll do what Ryzzi tells ya. Hear?" He squeezed her chin. "Ya hear?"

Struggling was useless. Mary let her body sag against him.

"That's better," he said.

As his hold relaxed, she lifted her head and spat in his face.

His eyes sprang wide as spittle ran down his cheek.

"Constable Peterson! Constable Peterson!" she cried, praying to be heard over the din. "Constable Peterson—"

Ryzzi grabbed her by the throat and pushed her to her knees. "Nobody can hear ya. Nobody cares." His grip tightened. "Only Ryzzi Kryzika cared, and now he don't care neither." He drew back a fist.

The door flew open, and the constable caught his upraised hand. "That'll be enough, Kryzika, or you'll be in jail yourself."

The man's frenzy died as quickly as it had been born. He danced back, brushed his suit of a phantom speck of lint. "I shoulda knowed better. She's nothin' but trash. I come here outta friendship to her husband. And what do I get for my trouble? The ingrate attacks me." He shook his head. "Can you believe it."

"Yeah, yeah." Constable Peterson looked skeptical as he shoved him out the door.

At the threshold the constable turned, casting his eyes on Mary, who was slumped against the bunk rubbing her bruised neck. "You all right?"

She turned away. If he couldn't see the truth when it was staring him in the face, what good would it do to tell him?

The officer paused, then shrugged, and slammed the cell door behind him.

Mary slumped again onto the bottom bunk, her cheek resting on the rough, grimy mattress. It smelled of mildew and sweat. Hopelessness dropped over her like a shroud.

Dear God, what was going to happen to her?

Maybe she should have made her deal with the devil after all. At least she'd have been out of this cesspool. But it was too late now.

Too late.

Drained, desolate, she closed her eyes.

If only she could wake up and find that it had been nothing but a bad dream. That it all had never happened. If only. . .

Half asleep, her mind played back the events that had led her here.

Her father's eyes were filled with rage as he lay at the bottom of the stairs, his leg twisted at a crazy angle beneath him. "I'll get you for this, boy. I'll get you."

And Brody, who'd pushed him, loomed on the landing above, sixteen and suddenly as big as their dad, breathing with a white-hot fury to match the old man's. "You'll not hit my sister again. Not as long as I'm here to protect her."

"By the saints, you'll not threaten me, boy," the old man roared, rearing up, then falling back in pain.

Behind the lad, fourteen-year-old Ethan stood, his eyes

wide and bright, horror-struck by the sight and inevitable outcome. They'd all be made to suffer for their brother's impulsive act. All three of them. Their father was indiscriminate in his thirst for retribution.

As if he needed an excuse.

From where she knelt beside him, Mary saw the neighbors' heads poke from doorways to see what all the ruckus was about, watched them gather into whispering clumps.

And she saw the understanding and compassion in their faces.

Mr. Button from the apartment next door lumbered over and put his arm around Brody's shoulder. "You'd better get out of here, son, or there'll be hell to pay with that daddy of yours."

"I'm not leaving my sister."

"Go," Mary commanded. "I'll be all right."

"No!" Brody stood resolute.

"You must."

As she rose, her father grabbed at her ankle. "It won't do no good. I'll catch up to him. He can't get away from me, by God."

But he had gotten away. He and Ethan—for good. All the money she'd managed to squirrel away for her own escape, she gave to them. She helped them pack and pressed the dollars into Brody's hand. "Take care of your brother," she said.

And she managed not to weep till they were out of sight.

The next morning at the factory, Ed McKenzie, in that lighthearted, jesting way of his, said, "Run away with me." The same as he had every day for the last month.

Mary was almost as surprised as he at her emphatic, "Yes!"

There was no longer anything to keep her there.

A week later they met at dawn on the dock, her excitement nothing compared to Ed's. Once he'd made the commitment, it seemed he could hardly wait to be gone. The gold strike in

Alaska had been his destination—until he met Mr. Ryzard Kryzika and learned the ship to South Africa's gold fields would set sail first.

Ryzard Kryzika. Ryzzi Kryzika. The name slithered around in her brain like the snake that he was. Fourth Street Ryzzi. . .

❧

Mary heard a key rattle in the lock.

After a moment of disorientation, the rancid odor of the mattress attacked her senses, and she opened her eyes. For a moment she pondered which was more miserable, her memories or the present reality.

Constable Peterson filled the doorway. "The magistrate wants to question you now."

She sat up.

The magistrate!

Nervously, she smoothed her skirt and tried to make a bun of her unruly curls with the few hairpins that hadn't fallen into the street during her altercation.

"Get a hustle on," the man said, dragging her to her feet. "He hasn't got all day."

Mary picked up the sad-looking little hat that had been stomped on, doing her best to reshape it, but with small success. Sighing, she placed it atop her head anyway. A lady was not seen without her hat and gloves, and having lost the latter, she'd have to make do with the former and hope the magistrate didn't notice.

"You've fussed enough." Constable Peterson pulled her out the door and up the narrow hall through the now familiar clamor of catcalls.

It was amazing what a person could get used to.

"Shut your faces, you louts." The cell block rang from the constable's nightstick striking the metal doors as he passed. "Blasted Boers are worse than the Blacks. At least the Kaffirs have sense enough to keep their mouths shut," he muttered, pushing and yanking Mary like some rag doll toward the stairs.

She suddenly grabbed the railing and refused to budge.

Despite her quaking heart and trembling knees, she'd had enough. The magistrate would think her a common criminal if she allowed herself to be treated like one. Besides, a girl had a right to her dignity. Even a poor girl.

"What now?" The constable frowned.

"You don't seem to realize," she said in a voice far more brave than she felt, "I'm perfectly capable of makin' it on my own without you draggin' me."

He gave an exaggerated sigh as if he were mightily put upon. But after a moment of enduring her steady gaze, he gave in. "Very well, but move along."

In front of an imposing door on the second floor, Constable Peterson paused and stiffened to his full height before he knocked.

"Come in."

Mary's heart pounded. She had no idea what to expect. A chamber of torture? In that instant, before the door opened, her imagination took flight, as did much of her courage.

She was greatly relieved, then, to step into a sunny, well-appointed office with nothing more threatening in view than the head of a strange, horned animal mounted on the wall behind the desk.

A man at the window turned as they entered. He was tall, fearsomely so, with a helmet of dark curling hair and stern features that she might have considered handsome had she not been so apprehensive. As he approached, she saw that he was not young, but not old either. And his eyes—his dark, intense eyes—seemed. . .perhaps. . .kind.

Constable Peterson shoved her forward and handed him a sheet of paper. "You'll note, sir," the constable said, "that this Mary McKenzie was accused of trying to steal a gentleman's wallet."

"Thank you, Peterson, I can read."

Mary protested. "But the man lied, sir. I didn't do it."

The magistrate quickly perused the paper, then looked at Mary. "Do you know what this says?"

"She signed it, sir." Constable Peterson pointed to Mary's signature at the bottom of the page.

The magistrate cast him an impatient glance. "I'm speaking to the young lady, Peterson. If you'll allow me." He turned back to Mary. "Do you know what you signed? Did you read this?"

There was something in his quiet voice and the gentle intensity of his eyes that made Mary incapable of pretending.

She hung her head and sensed in the ensuing silence that he understood.

"Fourth Street Ryzzi came to post her bail," the constable interjected, with a look that implied much more.

When he didn't finish the story, a rush of rage inflamed Mary. She drew herself up. Glaring at the constable, she said, "And I'm sure you'll also tell him that I'd have none of it." She looked up at the magistrate. "I'll have nothin' to do with that vile man."

"Even if it meant having him post your bail?" the magistrate asked.

Mary looked away, remembering the brief moment when she had wondered herself if she should have accepted Ryzzi Kryzika's offer. "Even then," she murmured.

"There's a pattern here, if you ask me," the constable said.

"Nobody asked you, Peterson," the magistrate responded through gritted teeth, clearly out of patience. "I'll handle this now. Thank you."

"But, sir—"

"That will be all."

. "But—"

"I'll take this up with you later, Constable."

In the wake of the magistrate's sharp retort, Constable Peterson's puffery fizzled like a deflated balloon.

Mary could not contain a momentary satisfaction as she watched him skulk from the office.

"Please sit down, Miss—"

"Mrs.—Mrs. Ed McKenzie."

The magistrate glanced at the sheet he held as if seeking confirmation—as if he, too, doubted she was married. Yet his manner was courtly as he escorted her to the chair in front of the desk.

He treated her like a lady.

Colin sat down across from the young woman and laid the sheet of paper on his desk. His eyes lowered again on the line Peterson had struck through "marital status," adding the single word, "questionable," and felt a stab of compassion for her.

Folding his hands, he leaned forward. "Now, Mrs. . . McKenzie. You tell me what happened."

Knowing what he had seen, he would now discover what he hadn't.

He observed her as she spoke, the sorry excuse for a hat that hid her burnished curls. She should let them fall free, he thought. . .if only she knew it. Poor little thing.

". . .leering and prancing," she was saying, "I didn't do nothin' to attract him. And what he said to me was disgusting, sir."

Colin was quite taken with the timbre of her voice. Even in her agitation it had a resonance and depth that could not be cultivated. It was captivating. "Go on," he encouraged.

"The masher'd seen me talkin' to that vile little Ryzzi Kryzika and he wouldn't believe that—"

And her mouth. Not a pouty little beesting that was so

much in fashion, but full, generous lips—

". . .he wouldn't believe I weren't one of Ryzzi's girls."

A mouth that murdered the King's English. Yet there was obvious intelligence in her face, and a dignity in her demeanor that he'd sensed even from a distance. "So then what happened?" he asked.

"Well, then the constable came. Constable Peterson, that is. After I hit the lecher and bloodied his nose. But Constable Peterson didn't believe me and. . .and. . ." She swallowed and tears filled her soft brown eyes, eyes that Colin suspected had seen their share of pain long before the trauma of this day. He reached into his vest pocket and pulled out a white linen handkerchief, which he extended to her.

Hesitantly, she looked at it.

"It's clean," he assured her.

"I knew that." She took it and daintily dabbed at her eyes and her charmingly tilted nose. "A gentleman like you wouldn't hand a lady a soiled handkerchief. It's just I was thinkin' how I'd return it."

Colin suppressed a smile. "We'll worry about that later." He leaned back. He couldn't remember when he'd enjoyed an interrogation so much—if ever. "So then Constable Peterson arrested you for petty theft."

She nodded, absently twisting the handkerchief between her fingers. "He asked me lotsa questions. But I don't think he believed my answers. . .and then I signed his paper." Her voice was getting smaller. "And he took me below." A shudder ran through her that made Colin's heart go out to her.

She lifted her gaze and a shy smile passed her lips. "I can't say I'd recommend the cleanliness here," she said softly. But the levity was soon lost, and he saw even more depressing thoughts reflected in her face. "What are ya gonna do with me?" she asked, her voice even thinner.

"How old are you, Mrs. McKenzie?"

"Nineteen."

The poor little bird, he thought. *The poor little vulnerable bird.*

He straightened in his chair and crossed his hands again on the desk. "First, I want you to know, I believe everything you've told me."

"You do?" Her voice quavered.

Well, almost everything, he thought. Without a ring or papers he had to share Constable Peterson's doubts about her phantom husband.

Then he told her about Henry and the telescope and how he'd observed the incident, but still had to hear it from her lips because there were things he couldn't know that only she could tell him. Then he smiled. "As for what I'm going to do with you, I haven't yet decided."

"You mean you're not gonna let me outta jail?"

He could see her fear. "Oh yes, of course. But I want to help you find a safe place to live. Johannesburg is too rough a town for a woman alone. And as I understand it, you aren't sure when you can expect your. . .husband. . .to return."

The young woman's shoulders sagged.

"Maybe we can find you a job," he said to encourage her. He looked down at the sheet on his desk. "It says here you sew."

She nodded. "I was the best at assembling sleeves in the factory. I have the scars to prove it." She smiled and held out her hand. "See my thumb? A sewing machine needle poked me when I was learnin'."

He shook his head sympathetically. "That looks nasty."

" 'Twas at the time, but it don't hurt no more. Serves as a reminder to pay attention to what I'm at."

As he gazed at her strong, useful hand, Colin couldn't help but be reminded of another that had impressed him not an hour ago, languid and pale, lifting a delicate teacup.

"And I'm good with children. I brought up my two brothers since they was four and six, when our mum died."

"In Johannesburg, that might be a more marketable skill than assembling sleeves," Colin said, an idea beginning to form. "It says on the sheet here that you're staying at the Anderson Street Hotel." The hotel had a reputation a cut below that of the jail, in Colin's estimation.

She nodded.

"I reckon we can find you a more suitable place than that. I'm going to talk to my friends, the Bryants. Emma, Mrs. Bryant, is with child, and she might appreciate a companion. It might even work into a permanent situation. What do you think of that, Mrs. McKenzie?"

"I'd like that," she said hesitantly. "I hope they take to me."

"The Bryants? Don't worry about that. I can almost promise you they will." He smiled. "They're very kind. And, like you, Americans. American missionaries."

"Missionaries?" She looked concerned. "I don't know if—"

"Don't worry," Colin said simply. "They don't judge. They just love."

"Well, I guess if they're friends a yours. . ." The young woman looked at him soberly. Finally, she said, "You're bein' so nice to me, ya really should just call me Mary."

"Aah. . ." It was the second time that day he'd been invited to call a lady by her Christian name. The comparison was enough to make him laugh out loud, and he did.

The girl looked distressed. "Did I. . .did I say somethin' presump—presumpt—"

"Presumptuous?"

She nodded.

"On the contrary. I'm honored. . .Mary." Of course he had no intention of inviting her to call him Colin as he had Grace Ellen Fitzsimmon. Still, he felt a keener pleasure in this innocent girl's candor than all the other woman's studied charm.

"Well, then." He slapped the top of his desk and rose. "Let's collect your things."

She did not move.

"Why the long face, Mary?"

"I doubt the hotel will let me take them without payin' what I owe. And Ed didn't leave me enough for that."

"How much is it?"

"Six pounds, at least."

"I think I can handle that," Colin said, rounding the desk.

She shook her head. "It wouldn't be right."

He put a reassuring hand on her shoulder and said gently, "I'm not Ryzzi Kryzika, Mary."

"I never said you was."

"I won't expect anything from you," he smiled, "except your good opinion." She was proud, this little one. He could see that. "And that you pay me back when you earn the money."

Her whole demeanor reflected her relief, and she broke into a smile that nearly blinded him. "You can count on that, for sure," she said, springing to her feet. "Oh, and Constable Peterson took my purse—"

"I'll see that you get it back."

As Colin escorted Mary to the door, she suddenly hung back.

"If I move in with your friends, how will Ed know where I am? He'll worry if he can't find me."

Colin tried not to show his impatience, but this was too much.

The blackguard had left her alone, in a foreign country, not only in debt, but in the care of the most contemptible of human beings, Ryzzi Kryzika. And she was concerned that he'd worry about her? Was she that dimwitted, after all?

Incredulous, Colin looked down into Mary's liquid brown

eyes and felt chagrined. She was innocent, not stupid. And very, very brave.

She needed his protection, not his condemnation.

four

Bouncing along in the two-seated carriage next to Magistrate Reed, Mary stared down at her clenched hands. She would never forget the look the desk clerk had given when the magistrate had requested her bill. The man's narrowed eyes. His knowing smirk. She would have enjoyed smacking that smirk off his soft pudden-face, as she might some pesky fly. Splat!

The magistrate had seen the look, too. "*Mrs.* McKenzie's bill." He'd repeated the "Mrs." in a no-uncertain tone, although Mary knew he was no more certain that she was a "Mrs." than the disbelieving desk clerk.

Mary's feelings for the magistrate were mixed. She welcomed his protection, was grateful for it, but deep down, anger simmered, for she could see he doubted her virtue.

Mary teetered and caught hold of the side rail of the buggy as the magistrate slowed for a vegetable cart that was crossing the street in front of them. Then he snapped the reins and clicked his tongue, encouraging the roan to resume its trot.

From beneath her bonnet, Mary's glance landed on the man's strong, gloved hands holding the reins with a loose, skilled assurance. Beside her, his knees jutted out twice as far as hers; he was that much taller than she. And he took up more than his share of space. Though she tried to be quite small and keep to her quarter of the seat, his shoulder kept brushing hers.

Concentrating on the road ahead, he looked intense, but not scowling or intimidating as when she'd first set eyes on him in his office. He was really very handsome, she thought, now that she had time to study him.

40

Stealing a glance, she noted his fine profile and patrician-straight nose, his generous, well-defined lips. Not pinched and mean like Constable Peterson, or pursed and stingy, like the desk clerk's. And, he had a strong chin.

She'd always thought Ed's chin rather weak. His least attractive feature and a sign of character she probably should have paid more attention to.

Shifting her gaze to the rutted, debris-filled street, Mary absently pondered her husband.

She'd liked Ed from the beginning. He'd made her laugh, and his devil-may-care charm lit up the dark humors of her own unhappy life. But love him? What did she know about love between a man and a woman? She'd seen little of it between her own mum and dad. At least Ed was a big improvement over her father. A pleasant man, Ed, she'd thought. A man she would learn to love.

But he'd run out on her before she'd had the chance, leaving her to rely on strangers.

Despite the magistrate's assurance, she wondered if she'd really be welcomed by the missionaries. What were these Bryants like? She'd always pictured missionaries as stiffly starched, judgmental people. Would *they* believe she had a husband? And if they did, what would they think of a girl who sailed off to South Africa and was married by a sea captain?

It might have been better to invent a good lie.

Her throat tightened, and she felt that clutch of desperation, the same as when she'd read Ed's note.

But he said he'd come back. And he would. He had to. To prove to Magistrate Reed—prove to everybody—that she—he'd been telling the truth. That she *was* Mrs. Ed McKenzie.

She gave a disconsolate sigh and felt the magistrate's gloved hand pat hers. A reassuring pat. The brown eyes that met hers were reassuring, too.

"Don't you worry, Mary. Everything's going to be all right."

He gave her hand a final squeeze and took up the reins again. "Trust me."

Oh, how she wished she could.

As she gazed into his kind, expressive face, hope lifted Mary's heart. Perhaps, at last, here was a man she could trust. *Why couldn't Ed have been more like you?* she thought.

"We're almost there," he said.

Mary had been so into her own contemplation that she had failed to notice the changing panorama. They were on the outer reaches of town now, the edge of the plain, where flat-top trees dotted the distant landscape and the sky was separated from the horizon by a string of mauve hills. The houses were larger and farther apart, trees blossomed and gardens flourished, and the air was redolent with the scent of flowers and new-mown grass.

The trotting horse slowed, then stopped in front of a white picket fence where an arbor of pink roses covered the gate.

A soft breeze caught the branches of a weeping willow at the corner of the white stucco house; its leaves, light as feathers, brushed across the lawn. Sky-blue shutters framed the windows, and yellow marigolds lined the garden path leading to the front door.

Mary's breath caught.

Surely they were not at the Bryants'. Her fortune couldn't have improved this much. Why, this was a heaven on earth. No, she could not see herself in such a place.

"Mary."

She heard her name as if from a distance.

"Mary."

She lowered her gaze and found the eyes of Magistrate Reed contemplating her with the same thoroughness that she had been contemplating the garden.

"We're here," he said, lifting his hand to assist her down the carriage steps. "We're at the Bryants'."

Still Mary hesitated. She felt as if she were in a dream—the man's encouraging voice, his dark, kind eyes and reassuring smile, the fairy-tale beauty of the surroundings. A feeling of trust and peace welled up from deep within her, and she, who rarely indulged in tears, felt again their sting.

Hesitantly, she placed her small, gloveless hand in his. She perceived the strength of his fingers grasping hers, and a shiver of excitement pulsed through her.

"Don't be afraid," he said, gently drawing her down.

"I ain't afraid." Her voice was harsher than she'd intended as she quickly retrieved her hand, suddenly more fearful of her confusing reaction to Magistrate Reed than the uncertainty of what lay before her.

But the magistrate seemed not to notice as he lifted her small satchel from the back of the carriage. Then, with the bag in one hand, his other at the small of Mary's back, he gently prodded her toward the trellised gate.

Barely had they passed through it when the front door flew open and a wiry man of medium height bounded down the steps. "Welcome, welcome, Colin." Arms outstretched, he greeted them with all the eagerness of one finding long-lost friends. A shock of straight dark hair fell across his brow, and behind thin, gold-rimmed glasses twinkled the most penetrating jet eyes Mary had ever seen.

"And this is Mary." He grasped her hands in both of his. "You are no disappointment."

How could he tell?

"So Peterson did his job," the magistrate said.

"Oh, yes." The man smiled. "He delivered your note."

And gave you an earful, I reckon, Mary thought.

Nevertheless, the missionary's greeting had been quite enthusiastic.

"If you haven't guessed, Mary," the magistrate said, "this is Reverend Bryant, overseer of the mission, and your host."

"Only temporarily, sir," Mary gave a small curtsy, "until my husband returns from the gold fields."

"For as long as necessary, my dear," the reverend said, taking the satchel from Colin and leading them up the path. "Mrs. Bryant is looking forward to a visit with someone from America."

"You're most kind, sir, and I'm very grateful." Mary hurried along, struggling to keep up with the energetic gentleman. "But I doubt where I come from would be of much interest." She thought of the tenement and the factory, and the squalid streets between.

The reverend stood aside and ushered her ahead of him into the entry hall. "Colin, you and Mary wait in the parlor while I find Emma."

Mary's gaze swept the moss green overstuffed furniture, plush-covered and fringed, that crowded the ample parlor. "Oh, my," she breathed. Matching brocade draped the windows and the walls, and, in abundance everywhere, were ferns and filigreed lamps. At her feet, a late afternoon sun dappled the Oriental rug. Truly, this was the most elegant room she could possibly have imagined.

She turned toward the magistrate, who stood a few feet behind her. "Oh, my." Her eyes glowed. "You never told me it would be so grand. That he would be so kind."

Magistrate Reed smiled. "And you have yet to meet Emma." He turned as an elegant woman swept into the room. "Speaking of whom—"

"My dear, welcome to our home." Mrs. Bryant's voice was cultured and melodic, her bearing statuesque, despite the fact that she was large with child. Mary noted that she was nearly as tall as her husband—quite tall, indeed—but at that, at least five inches shorter than Magistrate Reed.

Grasping the woman's extended hand, Mary replied softly, "Thank you, ma'am."

In contrast to the exuberance of her husband, there was a reserve in Mrs. Bryant that brought on a sudden shyness in Mary. But when the lady reached out and lifted Mary's chin and looked down with the kindest smile and warmest brown eyes, the warmest since—Mary glanced at the magistrate—since she'd looked into *his* eyes, her trepidation was swept away.

Mrs. Bryant turned and addressed a tall, angular young black girl about Mary's age, wearing a bright red wrap-around dress and an apron, who was standing silently in the parlor archway. "Please ask Nandi to prepare some lemonade, and perhaps a plate of cookies. Bring it out onto the terrace, if you will, Kweela. Thank you."

"Yes, Missus." The girl curtsied and disappeared as silently as she'd come.

"And now, my dear," Mrs. Bryant said, taking Mary's arm, "let me show you your room and give you a chance to freshen up."

Again, wonder challenged Mary's composure as the reverend's wife ushered her down the hall and into the sunny yellow room that was to be hers. A bright quilt embroidered with flowers of many soft hues covered the four-poster bed, banked at the head by at least a half-dozen pillows of varying shapes, sizes, and fabrics. On a narrow chest at the foot, Mary's dilapidated satchel looked even smaller and shabbier in these luxurious surroundings.

Mary walked over to a window that overlooked a vine-shaded verandah. Turning back, she noted a slipper chair and footstool that picked up a pink-checked fabric matching some of the bed's pillows. Next to it were a lamp and a table on which was arranged a small bouquet of marigolds in a silver vase.

Mrs. Bryant placed a hand on the chair. "A lovely spot to read."

Oh, dear. What would the woman think when she found out Mary couldn't read? That she was no match for this room?

Mrs. Bryant walked to the small carved chest beside the bed and picked up a leather-bound black book that lay next to the bedside lamp. "We left a Bible for you, although you probably have your own."

"No, I don't," Mary murmured, feeling like an impostor. A lump of discomfort had grown in her throat that she almost feared would choke her.

"Then, my dear, this is yours to keep," the woman said, returning it to the table and patting it like an old friend.

"Th–thank you." Mary could feel the flush burning her cheeks.

"Oh my dear, you mustn't be embarrassed." Mrs. Bryant rounded the bed and wrapped her arm around Mary's shoulders.

She can tell. Anybody can tell just by looking at me that I can't read.

"The Bible is a gift from God, to be shared. Now," Mrs. Bryant said briskly, "your closet is there, and next door," she took Mary into the hall and opened the door to an adjoining room, "this is the bathroom you will use. Ours adjoins our bedroom."

Mary's own bathroom? With a commode, a sink, and tub. And a *shower*.

Mary remembered the toilet at the end of the hall that served the six families on her floor of the tenement. . .and the shower in the basement that everyone in the building used.

"Now, you take your time, unpack, and join us on the verandah when you're ready."

"Thank you, ma'am." Awestruck by it all, Mary was still able to manage little more than a whisper.

"From now on you must call me Mrs. Bryant," the woman

said, leading Mary back to her room. "You are not a servant, dear, you are my companion."

When the door closed, Mary sank onto the bed, weak with fatigue. After the day she'd been through, her stomach roiled like the Coney Island roller coaster. She realized she hadn't eaten since breakfast, and then only a hard roll and a glass of tepid tea. But with all that had happened, the thought of food, even now, made her stomach churn.

In no more than a minute she had unpacked her mean little wardrobe. It took up less than a shelf in the lovely carved armoire. She shoved her satchel into the farthest, darkest regions of the ample closet and repaired to the bathroom.

A room of her own was more than she could ever have dreamed, but a *bathroom* all to herself, where she didn't have to wait in line, and where she could luxuriate in a shower that had cold and hot water, and where there was a full-length mirror where she could see down to her shoes—well, it was all just too much.

She washed her hands and face, then, studying her reflection, tucked back a recalcitrant curl and smoothed her bun. She frowned, not at all pleased with her hollow-eyed, pale reflection. If every time she looked into the mirror she was going to see such an anemic-looking sad-puss staring back, it might be just as well not to have one. She bit her lips and pinched her cheeks to add some color. That was the best she could do for now.

Returning to the parlor, Mary paused at the French doors leading outside. The verandah looked like a painting in a museum. Sunlight filtered through the canopy of a grape arbor onto the stone terrace. A set of wicker lounges angled toward the table set with china and silver. On either side of it sat the Reverend and Mrs. Bryant, while Magistrate Reed relaxed on one of the lounges.

At that moment, the servant girl came from what must

have been the kitchen, carrying a tray of tall lemonade glasses, sparkling with beads of moisture.

A cool, soft breeze carried the scent of citrus blossoms from dwarf trees in pots at the corner posts and tickled the leaves around fat clumps of fruit hanging heavy on the vine. The grapes looked ripe and luscious, and Mary was aware, once again, how long it had been since she'd eaten. She saw the little sandwiches and cookies delectably arranged on china plates and prayed her growling stomach would not give her away. She wanted to join the party, but shyness held her in the shadows.

"When are you leaving, Daniel?" Colin asked the reverend.

"In a couple of days. I have a baptism at Krugersdorp and then I'm going up north to visit the mines in the Murchison District. I'm not happy, Colin, about how the natives are being treated."

The magistrate laughed. "So you think you can wring some compassion out of the mining consortium?" Then he grew serious. "I hope you can. I wish you luck."

"I'd rather have your prayers." It was the reverend's turn to smile.

"I'll leave the prayers to Emma, thank you."

"You can count on me for that. I pray for the natives' souls . . .and yours," Mrs. Bryant added archly. She reached her hand across the small table and touched her husband's arm. "And I pray for you, my dear husband, always for you." She turned to Magistrate Reed. "I'm so proud of the work Daniel is doing here in Africa. So many lives have been changed."

The reverend's hand covered hers. "Oh, Emma, I couldn't do this work without the able assistance of my faithful, brave companion." His eyes met hers with such unrestrained love, it brought an empty ache to Mary's heart.

Oh, if only someone—if only Ed—looked at her with such devotion.

She gave a small sigh, which must have been louder than she'd thought, for all three on the terrace turned to see her standing there.

"My dear." Reverend Bryant rose.

To her surprise, the magistrate sprang to his feet as well, and before anyone else could move, he ushered her to a chair next to the lounge where he'd been seated.

Looking down at her, he frowned. "When did you last eat?"

"Not to worry, sir. I don't eat much." She glanced at the Bryants to assure them.

The magistrate rolled his eyes heavenward. "How could I have been so thoughtless—"

"For shame, Colin," Mrs. Bryant teased. "Why the poor little thing must be ravenous. Kweela," she said to the servant girl, who was standing by the table, "please prepare a plate for Miss—"

"Missus," Mary corrected. Obviously, that awful Peterson had not made it clear.

"Of course, my dear, I'm terribly sorry."

The woman looked so distressed, Mary hastened to add, "It makes no never mind. It's just I should set the record straight at the start."

"I'm glad you did, dear. Prepare a plate for Mrs. McKenzie, please," Mrs. Bryant repeated.

But while the exchange was going on, Magistrate Reed had already done so and now handed it to Mary along with a lovely embroidered, linen napkin.

"Oh, my, sir, I don't know if I can eat all this. As I said, my appetite ain't very big."

"Well, try," he commanded, clearly still chastising himself.

"Don't badger the poor thing, Colin. When she tastes Nandi's cooking, she won't be able to resist. Look at all the weight I've put on." Mrs. Bryant placed her hand on her belly, swollen with child, and chuckled.

She was hardly the stuffy missionary that Mary had expected.

And Mary did clean her plate, after all, which seemed to satisfy Magistrate Reed. When he finally rose to leave, she bounded to her feet. "You must tell me where to send the money I owe you, sir."

"Colin's a regular visitor, Mary," the reverend said, rising. "You won't have to worry about sending him anything. He comes to get his stomach filled with Nandi's fine cooking quite frequently." The missionary's eyes twinkled. "Emma and I pray that someday he'll accept some food for his soul, as well."

The magistrate grinned. "Watch out, Mary, these people are insidious. They never give up."

"Don't be so smug, Colin," Mrs. Bryant bantered, pushing herself to her feet. "Someday you, too, will recognize your need for the Lord." She kissed him on the cheek. "Will we be seeing you for supper before Daniel leaves?"

"By all means."

Over Mrs. Bryant's shoulder, Mary caught the magistrate's speculative gaze. On her.

She felt that same strange quiver of excitement she'd experienced when he'd helped her from the carriage. Lifting her hands to her burning cheeks, she lowered her eyes.

"Tomorrow evening, then," Mrs. Bryant said, linking her arm through the magistrate's as they all moved toward the entrance.

Mary followed, trembling with a confusion she could not comprehend.

As they gathered at the front door, the magistrate turned and searched her out. In a stride he was before her, taking her hands in his. His smile was warm and teasing. "You be a good girl, Mary."

"Not to worry about that, sir."

"If you need anything—"

"I'm sure I'll be quite fine. . .and I thank you, sir, from the bottom a my heart, for all you done." She lowered her gaze. " 'Course, you're the kind what woulda done it for anybody."

"Not so, Mary." Her lifted gaze locked with his. "Not so," he repeated softly.

It was only minutes after the door closed behind Magistrate Reed that an insistent pounding echoed through the house.

Mary's heart lurched. He was back.

The servant girl ran down the hall past Mary to the front door, Reverend Bryant on her heels, his wife close behind.

On the stoop stood a native, black as coal and taller even than the magistrate. He wore a bright orange-patterned loin cloth and carried a spear.

"Bokkie, what is it?" The reverend put his hand on the man's shoulder.

The African spoke quietly, and when he had finished, Reverend Bryant turned to his wife. "Chief Mlawu is failing. I must go at once."

"I'll help you pack, my dear." To Kweela, she said, "Take Bokkie to the kitchen, he needs something to eat and drink. And tell Nandi to prepare some sandwiches for the journey." With that, Mrs. Bryant followed her husband to their room.

Mary was in the parlor when the Bryants reappeared in the front hall. She knew it wasn't proper, but she couldn't help but watch as they bid each other farewell.

Their clasped hands. Her gentle caress. The lingering kiss he gave her.

How Mary envied them their kinship and regard for each other, and their tender expressions of love.

If only she had that with Ed. Oh, he'd expressed himself all right, but not with much tenderness. What love she'd felt for him waned when he'd spent every night of their voyage gambling. She soon realized he shared none of her dreams for a home and family—only for striking it rich and living the high life.

Maybe he'd sensed her disappointment. Maybe that's why he'd run off and left her.

Mrs. Bryant turned, her fine posture drooping as she pulled a lace handkerchief from her sleeve. Delicately, she wiped her eyes—and saw Mary.

"I always miss him so," she said, sparing Mary the embarrassment of getting caught observing such an intimate moment. She sighed. "But he must go. It's the Lord's work he's about." And then she brightened and reached out for Mary's hand. "But you, my dear, will keep me from being so lonely this time."

At least the kind lady was certain her husband would return. Mary had no such assurance about her own.

five

It seemed that no sooner had Mary's head hit the pillow and she'd closed her eyes, than she was yanked awake by what sounded like a hysterical human laugh just outside her window.

She bolted upright, her heart beating like the wings of a wild bird.

The weird, fiendish howl came again.

Leaping from her bed, Mary crashed into the armoire as she stumbled toward the door. Frantically, she fumbled for the knob and flung the door open.

At the end of the hall, Mrs. Bryant was silhouetted in the portal of her bedroom, tying the sash of her dressing gown. "Just a hyena, my dear, not to worry."

"Wh–what's a hyena?" Mary quaked.

"They're scavengers. Not at all interested in you and me." The woman stepped into the hall, linking arms with the trembling girl. "A frightful noise, isn't it? I reacted the same way the first time I heard it. What you need is a hot cup of tea," she said, drawing Mary toward the kitchen.

Sitting her down at the kitchen table, Mrs. Bryant filled a kettle with water, lit the flame under it, and piled a plate with cookies.

"Can't I help?" Mary asked, guilty that the mistress of the house worked while she sat useless.

"You just nibble on those, dear, while we wait for the water to boil." Mrs. Bryant settled across from her and helped herself to three cookies. "Now that I'm eating for two." She smiled and took a bite.

But Mary was still too nervous to nibble anything, even

one of the delicious-looking cookies. She jumped when a whoosh of wings brushed the eves just outside the kitchen window.

"The grassland is filled with wild creatures, especially since most of the big cats have been hunted down by *sportsmen*." Mrs. Bryant said "sportsmen" disdainfully.

"There are lions around here?"

"Not many anymore. They used to keep the animal population in check." Mrs. Bryant shook her head. "Now, it's up to the hunters who supply meat for the mines, I suppose."

The teakettle whistled, and Mary popped up to turn it off.

"Thank you, dear."

She poured the water into the teapot and brought it back to the table to steep. "Ain't it kinda hard to sleep with all them wild creatures?"

The lady smiled. "I thought it would be. But you get used to it. Out here on the edge of the plains, it's just part of the night."

"I don't think I'd wanna walk out alone after dark."

Mrs. Bryant laughed, a warm, easy laugh. "I think not. But then I won't walk alone in downtown Johannesburg in broad daylight."

Mary certainly understood that.

Before Mrs. Bryant poured their tea, she folded her hands and bowed her head.

Mary hesitated. In her family, if there was food or drink on the table, you'd better grab it before someone else did. But as the woman across from her began to speak, Mary, too, bowed her head and clasped her hands. At the rich tone of her benefactor's voice and the forthright trust of her words, a sense of peace came over her.

"Our Father in Heaven, thank you for the blessings of this day, and especially for bringing us Mary. We ask travel mercies for Daniel as he goes to dear Chief Mlawu. If it be thy will, we pray thee heal this good man, that he may continue to be your witness to his Lobedu tribe. Amen."

Mrs. Bryant raised her head and smiled into Mary's eyes as she lifted her cup.

Later, when they had parted for their respective rooms, Mary found that sleep was not as easy coming as before. It was not the noises of the plain now that held her, but her own sad thoughts. She was powerfully grateful for the kindness of these dear people, but knew she couldn't take advantage of their generosity forever. If Ed didn't return by the time she had paid her debt to Magistrate Reed, she must start saving for her return trip to America.

The breeze had stilled, and in the warmth of the night air, Mary pushed back her quilt and pulled the soft sheet up to her chin. She sighed, unable to quell the helpless sadness that was beginning to feel as natural as drawing breath.

❧

Mary's sleep was again interrupted, not by a screech, but by the twitter of birds in the arbor outside her window. She thrust aside the sheet, hopping out of bed with more vitality than she might have expected, and pushed back the drape.

The sun was just beginning to break over the distant hills, the soft light diffusing the verandah. Night sounds that had frightened her were now only an echo.

Still in her nightgown, she ran into the bathroom—her bathroom—pinching herself to be sure that wondrous luxury wasn't a dream. After dressing in the other of her two outfits, a beige skirt and faded blue shirtwaist, she combed her hair in front of the full-length mirror, pulling the unwilling strands into a tidy knot at her crown.

The house was silent as she tiptoed down the hall past Mrs. Bryant's room to the kitchen.

This morning she would show Mrs. Bryant what a help she could be. Donning an apron she found hanging in the broom closet, she put on a kettle of hot water for tea—it seemed that was all they drank in this country—and nosed through the pantry until she'd assembled the makings for biscuits. Once they were plopped into the oven, she strolled outside, teacup in hand.

Behind the main house was a large shed—for tools, she soon discovered—a stable, and a carriage house with living quarters above. She thought she saw a shadow pass behind the lace-curtained window.

As she wandered out past the kitchen garden toward the orchard, she paused, breathing in the rich sweet scent of newly turned soil, citrus, and roses. The rancid stench of jailhouse sweat and grease, the view of brick walls and barred windows were now the dream—the nightmare. This was the reality.

How lucky she was to be here. Or was it luck? Perhaps the God of her mother really did exist and was looking after her for her mother's sake. Her gaze lifted and, just in case, she prayed to that God to look after her brothers wherever they were.

Of course, Magistrate Reed had something to do with her good fortune. Without him she wouldn't be here. No matter what the future held for her, she would never forget that. . .or him. She looked toward the city and wondered if he, too, were awake. She remembered him as he'd been yesterday, about to leave, returning to her, her small hands lost in his—

"Wicked girl," she muttered. "You're a married woman. Don't you forget it." But his eyes had told her he, too, had forgotten—or did not believe that she ever was.

Mary swung back toward the house.

Such thoughts! Such imaginings! And at the risk of burning the biscuits.

Head lowered, she strode back to the house.

"What are you doing in my kitchen?"

The harsh voice brought Mary up short. She lifted her eyes to the angry ebony face of—she supposed—the cook.

"I say, what are you doing in my kitchen?" The woman, wrapped in an orange, native print dress, was fat and furious.

Mary's mouth went dry. "I was just—"

"I do not hear excuses. What are you doing? Trying to take my place?" Her *r*'s rolled out in a rumble, the native cadence of her voice making a discordant music.

"No, I—"

The cook wagged her finger under Mary's nose. "This is my work. You Missa Bryant's friend. A white lady. My apron!" She snatched it from around Mary's waist.

"But what can I do? I have to do something for my keep."

"You do what white ladies do." The cook sniffed, tying the strings of the apron around her own ample waist.

"Wh–what's that?"

"You sit on the verandah and drink tea." She began grabbing pots and clanging them together with enough racket and gusto to lead a marching band.

Obviously, there was no use in arguing. She wouldn't be heard if she tried. Disconsolately, she moved toward the door. "Don't let the biscuits burn," she managed.

"Biscuits!" the cook muttered disdainfully. "Those are not biscuits like I ever saw."

Abandoned yesterday. Banished today.

Mary peeked into the dining room and saw that the table was already laid for two, with more forks and knives than anybody needed and carved glasses that reflected rainbows on the polished wood table—not like the scarred one she was used to with the grime so deep no amount of scrubbing could make it clean again. There were roses in the middle in the shiny silver bowl.

Such luxuries. The Bryants were certainly not like the missionaries on the streets of New York, always poor and seeking funds for their ministries. Those had looked so pathetic and downtrodden, on occasion even Mary had felt obliged to give a donation.

It suddenly occurred to her, how did somebody behave at such a table? With so many choices, which fork should she use?

Instead of lifting her spirits, the beautiful room and sumptuous setting confused and depressed her.

A lady would know what to do. But what did Mary know about being a lady?

This was never going to work. She didn't belong here. She might just as well go in right now and pack her bags.

And she was about to do that very thing when Mrs. Bryant sailed into the dining room. "Good morning, dear." She planted a light kiss on Mary's cheek.

Used to being welcomed by her father's rabid glare in the morning, Mary was momentarily unsettled by the woman's affectionate greeting.

"You're up bright and early, Mary. Did you finally get a good night's sleep?" By now Mrs. Bryant was seated at the head of the table, her napkin in her lap. "Here, sit beside me. This will be your place. The reverend presides at the head of the table when he's here. I'm ravenous. I imagine you are, too."

"I don't usually eat much breakfast," Mary murmured as she reluctantly slid into the chair next to her hostess. What appetite she had, had diminished under the cook's wrath.

But that was not to be.

"A nutritious breakfast is essential to good health," Mrs. Bryant declared, ringing the small silver bell beside her plate.

The servant girl from the day before popped through the kitchen door.

"Good morning, Kweela. Will you please tell Nandi that we're ready for breakfast? Thank you, dear."

Mrs. Bryant bowed her head. "Our Father in Heaven, for what we are about to receive—"

To Mary's surprise, the girl paused by the door and lowered her head also.

Again, as Mrs. Bryant spoke, a transcendent calm came over Mary, and although her concerns still lingered, her despair seemed to lift.

"Kweela isn't a Christian, yet," Mrs. Bryant said after the girl had disappeared into the kitchen. "But I think she soon will be." She smiled. "She cleans and serves. Walks from her kraal every day—her native village," she added, explaining the African word. "I think she finds this job easier than caring for nine younger siblings."

Kweela returned to pour juice into the cut-glass goblets. She filled their teacups and covered the teapot with a cozy, then came back with two steaming bowls of porridge.

And that was just the beginning.

Platters of scrambled eggs appeared, followed by bacon, ham and sausage, fruit and cheeses, a silver holder filled with toast, butter, jam, and honey.

But no biscuits.

Mary could hardly taste any of it, she was concentrating so hard on copying Mrs. Bryant's every move, grateful that the hostess was always the one to be served first. Mrs. Bryant picked up a fork; Mary picked up the same fork. Mrs. Bryant cut her ham with the larger knife and spread her cheese with the smaller; Mary did likewise. She felt she was about to develop a nervous twitch, she was trying so hard.

Fortunately, her hostess seemed not to notice and chatted on without need of a response.

"Nandi and her husband Jalamba live in the quarters above the carriage house. Jalamba is our caretaker. They're both hardworking, honest. We count them among our blessings. When they first came, Nandi had a fearsome temper. But I'm happy to say, since she's come to Christ, her disposition is much improved."

Mrs. Bryant must have caught Mary's grimace. "You've met her?"

Mary nodded, not trusting herself to reply.

Her hostess chuckled. "I guess the Lord's work is never done. What happened?"

In the most delicate way she could manage, Mary explained.

Mrs. Bryant nodded sympathetically. "What a reception. You poor dear. The natives are covetous of their positions, and I can hardly blame them. There is so little decent-paying employment. That's why Daniel has given orders to provide food for anyone who shows up at our door. Nothing is wasted from our table." She frowned. "My dear, what's troubling you?"

"It's just. . .it's just. . .well, if Kweela cleans and serves and Nandi cooks, what is there left for me to do to earn my keep?"

"Why, my dear, didn't Colin explain? You're to be my companion."

Mary's brow wrinkled. "He said that, but. . .what exactly does a companion do?"

Mrs. Bryant put her elbows on the arms of the chair. "Before I was with child, when Daniel would be gone—weeks, sometimes months—I had my work to keep me occupied, even though I missed him dreadfully. But now, with my confinement, he has been pressing me to hire someone to help with my personal chores. More a friend than a servant. And to be honest, Mary, I really have not felt all that well during this time. When Constable Peterson brought Colin's note, we knew God was answering our prayers. And when he said you were a seamstress, with a new baby coming, well, that was an added blessing."

Mary's smile started small and broadened as Mrs. Bryant spoke.

"So you see, my dear, we need you as much as you need us."

Mary laughed lightly. "A bump and a bounce, that seems to be the way things have gone since I got to South Africa."

"With God's hands to catch you, you need not worry," Mrs. Bryant assured her.

Mary's smile warmed as she began to relax, really relax, for the first time.

"I especially need help catching up with my correspondence."

"Correspondence?" Mary's grip on her fork tightened.

Mrs. Bryant nodded. "So many letters come from America that need to be answered, and then there is the mission work, and some social correspondence. Speaking of that—" She clasped her hands and smiled. "Your first task will be a note to Colin to postpone our dinner until Daniel returns from Chief Mlawu's village." She folded her napkin and placed it beside her empty plate. "But we'll get to that later. Now, if you'll excuse me, I think I need to lie down. For some reason, I'm feeling a little weary."

Mary tried to speak, but no words came.

As she pushed herself to her feet, Mrs. Bryant glanced over at her. "What's worrying you now, my dear?"

She had to confess it. She had no choice. "I can't send your note to Magistrate Reed."

"Of course you can."

Mary slowly shook her head. "I can't write. . .or read," She added in an even smaller voice.

"What?" The woman looked aghast. "Why, that will never do."

As Mary rose, her shoulders slumped with the weight of the world. "I'll pack my things."

"And I lose my seamstress? Of course you won't! I am more convinced now than ever that God sent you." Mrs. Bryant looked almost gleeful. "I am an English teacher. I also tutor elocution and the art of public speaking—as well as the Bible, but we'll get to that later. Why, I'll have you reading, writing, and speaking perfectly modulated sentences in no time." She rubbed her hands together. "Daniel is in for a big surprise," she chortled. She took Mary's arm as they left the dining room. "And just for good measure, we might spruce up your wardrobe a bit. If you're going to be a proper companion, you should dress like one."

Mary's heart thumped, then soared as she envisioned herself in an elegant summer gown, serving tea on the Bryants' verandah.

Maybe Magistrate Reed would be there. Would he think her comely? As comely as the women in his world?

&

Colin gazed down at the street where he'd first seen his "little wren." He smiled. She was little enough, but hardly a wren, the way she'd so valiantly dealt with her attacker. She had more spirit and spunk in that petite body than all the supercilious society ladies put together. At least the ones he knew. He couldn't even imagine how Sylvia or the elegant Grace Ellen would have handled what that sweet soul had been put through. Was it just yesterday?

His musings were interrupted by a knock on his office door.

Deputy Magistrate Scott stuck in his head. "Mr. Higgins-Smythe is here to see you, sir."

"What now?" Colin groaned. The manager of the Johannesburg office of the Granger Mine was a constant irritant, making demands it would take a full-time army to handle.

The tall, bearded deputy rolled his eyes. "Problems at the mine."

"As usual. You'd think we were their own personal police force. That man expects us to send a full contingent every time a native blinks."

"I heard that, Reed." Bowler in hand, the rotund little man

in a casual three-piece suit pushed past the departing deputy. "And this time it's not the natives blinking, it's the foreigners." He sat stiffly in the leather chair in front of Colin's desk and balanced his bowler on his knee. "The outsiders are threatening to riot if the owners replace any of them with Kaffirs. If the company chooses to hire native workers, that's our affair. Foreigners have no right to tell us how to run our business—any more than the Boers did. That's why we fought the war."

"Not exactly." But Colin wasn't about to get into a discussion on the complexities of the bitter dispute between the Dutch and British settlers. This small-minded man wouldn't grasp it anyway. "So what do you want me to do from a hundred miles away?"

"Well," the man sneered, "you might send a contingent."

Colin sat down behind his desk. "Has the company tried arbitration?"

"The owners feel it's gone beyond that." The man rose abruptly. "They have authorized me to demand your immediate response. As taxpayers—*generous* taxpayers—they expect order to be restored."

Colin stood up. He hated to give in to the offensive little man, but the Granger operation was a major voice in the mining consortium, giving them considerable political clout. As a public servant, he was forced to pay attention. "Very well, I'll get on it."

"At once!" the man commanded. He turned at the door. "This morning!"

Colin sighed. He'd have to cancel dinner at the Bryants'. That was a disappointment. He looked forward to Nandi's cooking, to say nothing of his conversations with Daniel, who he considered to be one of the most stimulating, erudite men he'd ever met. And Emma was just as challenging. They were a rare couple.

And, of course, there was Mary. He wondered how the brave little soul was faring.

He called in his second-in-command and grudgingly issued his orders for departure, then lifted his military cap from the hat tree. "I'll stop by the Bryants' on my way out of town."

❧

Dust rose from the horses' stamping hooves as Colin and his company of men detoured down the road to the Bryants' house later that afternoon. He had twenty—a third of them black—all good men and true.

As he rode along, Colin wondered what encouragement he could give Mary when he saw her. The interview he'd had that morning with Ryzzi Kryzika in the man's cesspool of a brothel had confirmed that she'd traveled on the Southern Star with an Ed McKenzie. Kryzika's description of the man fitted that of Mary's. Anger boiled in Colin even now, thinking of the shifty-eyed procurer, surrounded by the blowzy, coarse women he employed, referring to sweet, clear-eyed Mary as "uppity tenement trash." It had been all Colin could do to keep from grinding his fist into the fellow's pugnacious face.

Colin rode ahead, dismounting at the gate, his men coming to a halt behind him. As he walked up the front path, Emma opened the door.

"Colin, I was just about to send you a note."

Nandi's husband, Jalamba, came hustling around the side of the house, and Colin noticed that two other dark faces looked past the parted curtains of the parlor window. Nandi and Kweela giggled at his smart salute. It wasn't every day twenty men, uniformed and armed, appeared at the missionaries' door.

"Good heavens, what's all this about?" Emma clasped her hands, looking at the company in bewilderment.

Colin grinned, searching for Mary and finding her in the

shadows of the entry. "Just thought I'd bring the regiment along for dinner. Daniel being famous for his miracles, I reckoned he could provide—rather like the loaves and the fishes. Don't you think?" Over Emma's shoulder he smiled at Mary.

"Why, Colin," Emma bantered, "I didn't realize you'd become a biblical scholar. Daniel is gone."

"Oh?" With some effort, Colin pulled his gaze from the young woman.

"Last evening, just after you left, one of the natives from the Lobedu Kraal appeared at our front door."

"Chief Mlawu?"

"He's worse."

"I'm sorry." Colin lowered his eyes to the cap he was rotating in his hands. "I'm on my way to the Granger Mine." He looked up. "I'll stop by and pay my respects. Do you have a message for Daniel?"

"Only, Godspeed."

Mary cleared her throat, and Colin's gaze darted again to her sweet face.

She stepped forward. "I don't suppose there's been any word from Ed?"

Oh, those soulful, searching brown eyes, so hopeful. Married or not, how could the cad have given her such shabby treatment? Colin shook his head. "I'm sorry. . .perhaps, on this journey to the mines, I'll run across him."

Her pained, brave expression wrenched his heart.

Colin grabbed her hand. "I'll find him for you, Mary. I promise." But wrapped in the warmth and trust of her gaze, he suddenly realized it was a promise he wasn't at all sure he wanted to keep.

Emma put her hand on Colin's arm. Reluctantly, he turned and saw in the woman's eyes recognition, and a gentle warning.

"We'll have a feast when you and Daniel return. And, God

willing," she added, "you'll bring good news from Mary's Ed."

"God willing," Colin murmured. And under Emma's discerning watch, he put on his billed cap and strode back down the path.

He motioned his column to move forward, and although he vowed not to, he looked back.

Mary raised her hand in a gesture of farewell, and he imagined that her eyes reflected the same longing he'd tried not to show in his own.

six

Shortly before noon the next day, Colin pulled up at the rise of a small hill and looked down over the conical-roofed reed huts surrounding the central corral of one of the few remaining kraals in South Africa. The fence circling the native village was in disrepair, and he sensed, even from where he sat, the despair and discouragement of a people and their country exploited by the likes of himself. He felt a moment's shame.

Motioning his men to remain behind, he pressed his heels against the stallion's flanks, and the horse broke into a slow trot down the slope toward the tall, yawning entry.

To his surprise, he saw Daniel, leading his sorrel gelding toward the gate. Beside him strode Chief Mlawu's son, Ntsikana.

Lean and tall as an ebony tree, Ntsikana was wrapped in a leopard-skin cloak. A pelt banded his broad brow, from which waived a long, thin feather. He was wearing the trappings of chief.

Chief Mlawu was dead.

Colin's heart sank. He reined his horse to a walk.

Daniel raised a hand in greeting, but his face was drawn, and now a deeper concern etched his features. "Colin. What brings you here? Is there a problem at home?"

"No, not at all. Emma is fine. They're threatening an uprising at the Granger Mine. I'm on my way there. But when Emma told me the chief had taken a turn for the worse, I hoped—" He avoided Ntsikana's eyes. "I thought maybe there was something I could do to help."

"You help?" Ntsikana, standing just behind Daniel, spat

into the dirt. "You are a chief with no teeth, except when you turn your guns on my people." His voice was resonant, and he spoke with an Oxford accent.

The animosity between him and Colin ran as deep as their college ties, for they had once been friends. But no longer. Colin's heritage was British, and Ntsikana had come to hate all that was British, including his old friend. Now, in his piercing black eyes, all his anger, hate, and frustration over the years of his people's subservience to the white intruders simmered in a brew that threatened to boil over.

Colin suspected that only Daniel's calming presence managed to keep a lid on the pot.

But, although the grieving man did not lift his spear, his fury could not be silenced.

"What lies will they promise now at the Granger Mine? Will they force the Kaffirs to sign more contracts that they, themselves, do not keep, then, as always, forbid my people to quit and go home? Will they go on promising to send for the workers' wives and children and pretend the words were never spoken? Will they continue to charge so much for lodging and food at the mine-owned stores that there will never be enough left over to send home to their starving families?"

Ntsikana rose to his full, imposing height. "Now that I am chief, not one man from my village will go to work in the mines. I will thrust a spear into his heart first!"

For a moment there was silence. Then Daniel put his hand on the man's tightly muscled arm. Quietly he said, "My friend, your concerns are mine." He glanced at Colin. "And Magistrate Reed's. I know that for a fact. We have discussed it many times."

Ntsikana grunted, proud and disdainful, still disbelieving.

Daniel continued. "We, he and I, unite with you in your mission for reform." Again he glanced at Colin. "That is why I am joining the magistrate on his journey to the mine."

Oh, no. Colin loved Daniel—like a brother. But he certainly didn't need a Bible-thumping missionary where he was heading, not that Daniel was the meddling kind. But there was nothing Daniel could do to help with the impending problem at the Granger Mine. Except get in the way.

২৯

Mary sat in the rocker hemming the baby dress she'd stitched while Emma played the piano.

In all of her nineteen years, Mary had never been so happy, nor at peace. . .to say nothing of feeling so suitably stylish. Mrs. Emma had taught her how to do her hair just so, parted in the middle with soft waves, and her curls pulled into a cluster at her crown. And Mrs. Emma had given Mary several lovely dresses from her own wardrobe that the two of them had refitted for Mary.

Mary sighed, smoothing the skirt of the lavender piqué shirtwaist she was wearing. Mrs. Emma had such impeccable taste. She was always dressed just right for the occasion. And she had such elegant manners. Mrs. Emma never hesitated about which fork to use. . .and now, neither did Mary.

Mary bit off the end of the thread and smoothed the tiny garment on her lap.

She loved listening to Mrs. Emma read the Bible each night and to her direct and simple prayers at mealtime. She even enjoyed going to church with her—the bonnets that Mrs. Emma let her borrow made her feel quite fashionable, although sometimes the deacon's sermon got a little long. And she wasn't the only one who thought so. Last Sunday she'd overheard a couple of the ladies whispering that they could hardly wait until Pastor Bryant returned to the pulpit.

Sometimes, after the service, she'd go with Mrs. Emma to visit folks who were sick or in trouble, and Mrs. Emma told her how she, Mary, had a natural gift for lifting people's spirits.

And twice Mrs. Emma had taken her to the dry goods

store to purchase lovely pastel fabrics and laces to make dresses for Mary. And the baby, of course.

As Emma played "Rock of Ages," Mary glanced warmly at the woman who, in the last four weeks, had become more than a mentor. She'd become a dear and cherished friend. She'd been so encouraging and patient, and as a result, Mary's progress had been phenomenal—or so Mrs. Emma said. It was amazing how quickly a string of letters had turned into words she could read, and if she didn't know the word, Mrs. Emma had taught her how to sound it out. She'd banished "ain't" from her vocabulary. . .except when she forgot, and she didn't end sentences with a preposition. . .most of the time.

When the anthem came to an end, Emma thumbed through the hymnal again. Then, lowering her hands to the keyboard, she began to sing in a spirited voice, "Come to the church in the wild wood—" She nodded at Mary to join in. "—Come to the church in the vale. No place is so dear to my childhood as the little brown church in the dale."

Mary rocked back in her chair, laughing with happiness. Mrs. Emma had taught her many of the beautiful old hymns, but she knew this was Mary's favorite.

Emma began again, this time singing a descant, "Come, come, come, come—" while Mary repeated the melody.

When they had finished, Emma rested her hands in her lap. "Mary, you have an absolutely *beautiful* singing voice. Matched by an almost perfect natural sense of phrasing."

Mary couldn't hide the pleasure she felt at the compliment. Mrs. Emma never hesitated to praise Mary's accomplishments, to the point that Mary was afraid she might get overly used to such lovely treatment and expect it always. She knew very well, when Ed came back, she wouldn't get such appreciative responses from him. Even though he expected them from her.

Ed. Now why did she have to think about him right now?

She was making such progress, learning so much every day. But the more she learned, the more she realized how much more there was to know. When Ed came back, it would all be over. And that made her sad.

"It's just not fair to hide your talent under a bushel," Emma said. "I've decided! You, my dear, will join our musicales."

Mary put down her stitching. "What exactly is a musicale?"

"It's when folks get together to play music. We try to manage at least once a week, which, unfortunately, rarely happens, given the demands on Daniel and Colin."

"Magistrate Reed comes to your musicales?"

Emma nodded. "Colin plays the violin, Daniel, the flute, and I, the piano. Colin's friend Henry learned the cello just so he could join us." Emma smiled. "Henry has plenty of time to practice. His wife Sylvia is our audience."

"I see. Of course. I'd be happy to be part of the audience," Mary said brightly. "That doesn't sound too hard. All you have to do is smile and clap."

"No, no, dear Mary," Emma chuckled, "you will sing."

"In front of other people?" Mary was horrified. "I couldn't possibly."

"But of course you can. You sing for me, don't you?"

"But you love me. With you it doesn't matter if I make a mistake."

"We all make mistakes, dear. Besides, everyone who meets you loves you."

Even Magistrate Reed?

Mary hoped Mrs. Emma couldn't read her mind. They were bad, bad, the thoughts she had of Magistrate Reed. They frightened and shamed her. As she did with thoughts of Ed, she tried to push them from her mind. But with far less success.

And they came at such odd times, like when she watched a beautiful sunset, or smelled a rose, or tasted something sweet. For no reason at all he'd come into her mind.

And now she wouldn't even be able to listen to Mrs. Emma play the piano without thinking about him. Oh, it was so painful.

Yet, she found a perverse pleasure in the pain that was both mystifying and compelling.

"This will be perfect," Emma chortled. "I received a note from Sylvia Harcourt last week. She has a friend she wants to bring along who sings. The two of you can perform duets."

"No, no," Mary said with feeling. "Not me!"

"Not *I*, dear," Emma corrected absently. "Of course, you'll do it. You will be wonderful. I have all the confidence in the world." She swung around on the piano stool, then rose, abruptly, awkwardly.

And screamed!

The dissonant crescendo rang out as Emma fell back against the keyboard. "Oh, dear God, dear God. Oh, Mary, help me," she cried. Clutching her distended belly, she reached out toward the horrified girl.

❧

Colin took a swig of water, rescrewed the cap on his canteen, and hooked it back on the pommel of his saddle.

The landscape had grown more tropical, lush, and green as they'd traveled north, the air humid. Monkeys swung from the limbs of the trees, and vibrant-hued birds squawked and chattered in the branches above them. In the last few days, they'd passed a colorful patchwork of prosperous plantations—bananas, coffee, sugar cane, cotton.

But in stark contrast they now approached a sprawling city of shacks set against the ripped and gouged earth of the mine field. Even from a mile away, Colin could hear the dull thud of the stone crushers in the stamp mills.

He glanced at the wiry, athletic man riding beside him. For a starched-collared missionary from America, Daniel had shown his mettle more than once these past few weeks. He looked tan and fit as any of Colin's own men.

"Has the midday sun beaten you into silence?" Colin asked his usually loquacious companion.

Daniel returned a guilty smile. "I was thinking of Emma. Sometimes, in my zeal to do the Lord's work, I'm afraid I neglect her."

"This from the man who at every stop composes long letters to be sent home?" Colin shook his head.

"I miss her. And now, with it so close to her time, I'm nagged by the feeling that she needs me."

"Don't fret, old man," Colin said, shifting in his saddle. "Nandi and Jalamba will take good care of her. And Mary McKenzie seems like a kind, sensible girl."

"But so young and inexperienced."

"I dare say, she's seen more of life's sadness than most her age." Colin pictured Mary's glowing, innocent face, aged by eyes shadowed with sorrow.

"It's a shame, in the eight mines we've visited, no one has heard anything of her husband," Daniel said.

Colin's hand tightened on the reins. Daniel's words brought a distasteful reminder of the girl's source of pain. "The greedy fool probably struck out on his own. He'll find out soon enough that the easy-to-reach gold is gone. Since he's not experienced, he'll end up in one of the mines laboring for wages less than what he made in America." Then how could he take care of Mary? For her sake, Colin quashed unworthy thoughts of the man's demise. He didn't wish him dead, just gone. Forever!

"Even if he does get a job in the mines, there's no guarantee he'll keep it," Daniel said. "As we saw at the Granger, white men are being replaced by the cheap native labor." He shook his head. "Alas, this trip has served to prove Ntsikana more right than wrong."

"No wonder he's rejected the white man's God his father embraced. Ntsikana has seen sorry little of the Christian charity you missionaries preach about. Your Lord might be better served if He'd called you to teach brotherly love to your white parishioners, instead of instilling useless hope in the innocent natives."

"Don't blame God for man's inadequacies," Daniel reproached, then added ruefully, "but you have a point."

"Thank you."

"Which only goes to prove, no man is without need of the Lord, regardless of color, or station. . .even a magistrate."

By this time they had reached the edge of the first gaping hole, and Colin's retort was lost in the clatter and clang and thundering thumps of machinery. He halted his squad on the perimeter and stared down, watching the scores of men, mostly black, bare to the waist, sweating in the heat of the tropical sun as they stripped the earth and wheeled the rock toward the stamp mill, where white operators crushed it into gravel from which the gold would be extracted.

Daniel pulled that infernal starched collar and black coat from his saddlebag. "I hope we can make some inroads here," he said, the eternal optimist.

Wheeling his horse, Colin shouted, "Sergeant, have the men bring their mounts into line. Look smart as we ride in."

In formation they trotted past the rude bunkhouses, shanty stores, and sheds toward the headquarters, a one-story building, not much more substantial than the rest, with a covered porch running its length.

In the shade lounged a group of khaki-clad white toughs, silently watching the brigade approach. Against one of the precarious-looking posts that held up the roof leaned a giant of a man, his pith helmet pulled down over his eyes. Absently, he played with the handle of the pistol in his unstrapped holster. As the contingent pulled to a halt, he spat a wad of tobacco into the dirt in front of them.

This was the second time that had happened to Colin on this trip. It seemed he was no more welcome here than he'd been at the Lobedu Kraal, where Ntsikana had spit at the sight of him.

He glanced at Daniel. If these men were spoiling for trouble, he certainly didn't want his friend involved. This sort of thing was precisely why he had tried to discourage him from coming along.

But as these thoughts crossed his mind, a man in shirt-sleeves and baggy, brown pinstripe trousers held up by a pair of black suspenders stepped through the office door. "After-noon," he said. Sweat beaded his face, and he wiped the back of his neck with a soiled handkerchief. "What can I do for you?"

"Just out on patrol," Colin answered. "Any problems?"

"None that our 'bully-boys' here can't handle." The man grinned at his surrounding crew and then back at Colin. Shielding his eyes, he spotted Daniel and moved off the porch toward him. "I say, might you be the Reverend Bryant from Johannesburg?"

"I am."

"Aye, you fit the description all right. Had a bloke out here a couple a days ago, said you might be heading this way—"

Colin had a sinking premonition. "Was there a message?"

"Aye." The man seemed to be taking a perverse pleasure in taking his time. "There was."

Colin straightened. "Well, what is it, man? Speak up."

Daniel grasped the reins with such a grip his knuckles turned white. "I'd be obliged—"

"Don't think so, when you hear your wife's been taken sick. Suppose by the time you get back, though, whatever her complaint, the crisis will be passed."

Daniel's face turned ashen.

It was all Colin could do to keep from removing his booted foot from its stirrup and ramming it down the mine manager's throat.

Without warning, Daniel snapped his reins and was wheeling his mount when Colin grabbed hold of the bridle.

"Don't be a fool, man. You can't just take off on a spent animal. Besides, it's not safe, a man traveling alone." He turned to the mine manager. "We need four fresh horses. The best you've got." To his men, he barked, "Avery and Stowe will come with us. Sergeant Knox, you're in charge. Rest the men overnight and follow in the morning."

"How do you expect to get our horses back to us?" the mine manager whined.

"Send a couple of your bully-boys with my men." The glint in Colin's eye brooked no argument. He looked over at his friend, who sat still as a stone, his head bowed. Only his lips moved.

Colin's jaw tightened. He clenched his fists, wanting to shake them at a God who could allow this pure and dedicated servant to suffer such despair.

He saw himself as a lad of eight, standing by the bedside of his own mother great with child. Praying. Oh, how he'd prayed for her. But God had not listened to a small boy's prayers.

His mother had died. And so had the baby that had been his brother.

That's when Colin had stopped believing in God.

He touched Daniel's arm and said gently, "Dismount, old man. We need to remove your saddle."

seven

Gently, Mary smoothed back the soft, brown hair waving around Emma's brow. How beautiful she was. How peaceful in sleep. And why not? Emma's prayers had been answered. That very afternoon, the doctor had visited and pronounced her finally out of danger.

Mary picked up the sleeping woman's tray from the bedside table. The trick would be to keep Mrs. Emma in bed. She was usually so active.

Mary had been amused when she'd discovered how upper-crust society ladies were usually confined to their homes once it was obvious they were with child. In the "society" in which she grew up, the "ladies" had no such luxury.

But confinement had not stopped Mrs. Emma. Not only had she attended Sunday services, she'd continued teaching her Bible classes, albeit in her own parlor instead of at the mission church. And the little ones still came for piano lessons. And there were still reams of correspondence to get through every week—to say nothing of all the extra attention Mary's lessons required. And finally—Mary got tired just thinking about it all—Mrs. Emma had insisted on continuing to take instruction in German, of all things. She said she wanted her mission to embrace the Boers, as well as the natives and the British.

The woman was a saint, but something had to give. And Mary was bound and determined to see that from now on Mrs. Emma did what was best for her and the baby.

She tiptoed to the bedroom door, closing it softly behind her as she went, and carried the tray into the kitchen.

"I could have done that, missy." Kweela jumped up from the table, where she and Nandi were sharing a pot of tea, and tried to take the tray.

"You just stay put, Kweela, you're as tired as I am, and you still have that long walk home." Mary nudged the girl aside as she carried the tray to the sink. "I think I'll ask Jalamba to hitch up the mare and take you in the buggy."

Sinking into a kitchen chair, Mary poured herself a cup of tea and refilled theirs. She saw their mild surprise—*she* was serving *them*—but pretended not to notice as she reached for one of Nandi's fresh-baked sugar cookies.

She had to be careful, though. In this stratified society they each had their place, and Nandi, especially, felt more comfortable if the lines were not crossed. Mary had found that out the hard way, on her first day.

"Mmmm." She chewed the cookie appreciatively. "How you had the energy to make these is beyond me. And the way you've taken care of Mrs. Emma, plus doing all your other chores, is amazing. You, too, Kweela."

"We are all in this together, missy." Nandi rubbed her arthritic knee. "You have done more than your share, too."

Not in the prayer department.

Mary had never seen anything like the servants' constant and fervent praying. Even Kweela prayed as loud and long as the other two. They couldn't have been more impassioned had Mrs. Emma been their own flesh and blood. They'd even enlisted Jalamba to gather other members of their family to join them in their earnest supplication to the Lord. In fact, their zeal had been so enthusiastic, the doctor feared they would disturb the patient and begged them to disperse.

But the trust and devotion that Mary had witnessed in these earnest people had made her aware of her own spiritual inadequacy.

"What did the doctor say?" Nandi asked.

Mary helped herself to another cookie. "He says she's out of the woods."

Kweela, whose name translated meant "jump up," did just that. "Oh, no, missy. It is too soon. Missy Bryant cannot go into the woods yet."

Nandi grabbed Kweela's skirt and yanked her back into her chair. "She said out of, not into." Then she rolled her eyes at Mary. "The girl is not so smart."

Kweela slapped her arm. "That is not nice."

Pushing her hand away, Nandi turned to Mary. "So, what is it that you mean?"

Mary suppressed a smile behind her lifted cup. "It means, Mrs. Emma is no longer in danger of losing her baby."

"Oh, glory be." Nandi closed her eyes and lifted her hands. "Praise the Lord."

"Thank you, Jesus," Kweela cried, eyes closed, upraised arms swaying from side to side. For not being a Christian, she was certainly sounding like one.

Tears ran down their blessed faces as they cried out their praises and prayers.

Mary watched, not quite sure what to do.

Suddenly, the back door slammed.

As one, their heads turned and their gazes fell on a stooped, disheveled stranger. The three froze. Then Mary realized it was Reverend Bryant.

"Oh, God. Oh, dear God. I'm too late." The voice that had power to move the masses trembled, weak with fatigue and despair. The reverend braced himself against the table, tears coursing down his stubbled cheeks.

Realizing he was misinterpreting the scene, Mary sprang from her chair. "You're dear wife is fine—" But the blood suddenly rushed from her head. Her vision blurred and she reached out toward the table for support. In the background, she thought she heard the door slam again, but the sounds around her melded into a faint buzz as she felt herself falling.

Strong hands grasped her arms, easing her back into the chair. From a distance she heard a voice urging her to lower her head and felt the firm but gentle pressure of a hand pressing her head to her knees.

"All I need is *two* sick ladies on my hands." Nandi's husky voice penetrated Mary's fog of consciousness.

"Are you all right?"

The deep, familiar voice took her breath again. And as her vision cleared, she found the worried face—dirty, unkempt, and handsome as she had ever seen—of Magistrate Reed, who was kneeling beside her.

"Missy is doing just fine. The baby, too," Nandi was assuring the reverend. "No need for you to go back and be waking her up, now that she is finally asleep." But her last words were lost on Reverend Bryant, who had already bolted through the kitchen door. Turning her attention on the magistrate, she said, "You look pretty undone yourself."

But Magistrate Reed seemed not to hear as he knelt beside Mary, his gaze still on her face.

He was so close she could see the damp curls pressed to his forehead, and each worried furrow, each hair of his expressive brows, each lash fringing his dark eyes and the pupils within. She could see each line of laughter, etched light in his tanned skin. Each bristle in his unshaven cheek.

Kweela leaned over his shoulder and peered into Mary's face. "Missy looks as pale as if she fell into a lake of leeches."

"She does," Nandi agreed, her mountain of flesh forcing Kweela aside. "You rest, girl, before we need take care of you, too."

"I think that's a very good idea, Nandi," the magistrate murmured. Rising suddenly, he scooped Mary into his arms. "Which way is your room? I'm taking you to bed."

She seemed light as feather down, light as an armful of roses and smelling as sweet. The rich amber curls that Colin had only seen confined in a tight knot on Mary's crown hung loose and free around her upturned face. They brushed across his cheek, tickling the tip of his nose.

"Please, sir, put me down," Mary protested. "I'm fine, now, perfectly capable of walking."

"Just tell me which is your room, and I will." Perhaps it was wishful thinking, but he perceived her struggle to be less than resolute.

She sighed, "Across the hall from the parlor," and seemed to sink quite naturally against his chest.

He wondered if she could feel that her small gesture had caused his heartbeat to accelerate.

Still holding her, for he knew this moment would end too soon, he managed to turn the knob and pushed open her bedroom door with his booted foot. He carried her to the bed and laid her gently on the flower-embroidered comforter. It took all the strength of will that he could muster not to reach out and touch the lustrous tresses that now spread across her pillow.

He took a step back. "You're sure you're all right? I mean, you don't need help in getting into your nightclothes—"

Mary's eyes widened.

"I meant, should I call Kweela—" What had this girl done to him? He was acting like a blathering idiot.

"No, thank you, sir," Mary said primly, pushing herself up into a sitting position. "I'm sure I'm fine now. Thank you, sir."

He took two more steps back and cleared his throat. "Well. . . you get a good night's sleep. You need not worry about Emma tonight. Daniel will take proper care of her."

"I'm sure you're right about that, sir."

Tired as he was, Colin still couldn't seem to draw himself away. "She's lucky to have had you here, Mary."

"She ain't—ah—isn't the lucky one, sir, it's me—" Mary frowned. "Or is that 'I'?"

Colin tried not to smile. She was so sweet and innocent, and lovely.

Mary shrugged. "Anyway, aside from this difficult time, which now seems to have passed, these have been the happiest weeks of my whole life. . . And I owe it all to you, sir. I'll never forget that."

There was a special warmth in the soft timbre of her voice. And he was quite sure that he was not misinterpreting the regard that shone in her expressive brown eyes.

"You must sleep now. I'll return tomorrow to visit Emma."

And you.

"Before you go, sir—"

"Yes?"

"Did you hear any news of Ed?"

Mary's question doused Colin's heated thoughts like a splash of cold water. Oh, he was sure she was anxious to know about the phantom Ed McKenzie, but was her question also a subtle reminder of propriety?

Whether or not that was her intention, it served the purpose. "I'm sorry." He shook his head. "No one has seen or heard of him. At least not in the mines we visited. Of course, it's always possible he struck out on his own."

Mary nodded. "That sounds more like Ed. He said he didn't come to South Africa to work for wages. He expected to make a big strike on his own." Then she seemed to sink down into herself, her sad thoughts removing her from Colin. "Thank you, sir. I know you did your best," she added absently.

"I'll keep trying," he promised, though he doubted she'd heard him.

That blackguard, Colin thought, marching out the door.

That fool. When Ed McKenzie left Mary, he'd left something of far greater value than the richest vein of gold.

❧

Mary wasn't as innocent as she suspected Magistrate Reed believed. She'd felt his beating heart and seen the yearning in his eyes. As she stared at the closed door, she pictured him, covered in dust and weary. What an extraordinarily handsome man he was, matched only by the most sterling qualities of character. Trustworthy, loyal, compassionate. Certainly not qualities she'd seen in her father. Or Ed. Before she met Magistrate Reed, she'd begun to despair that they even existed.

What wonderful people surrounded her in this place. Was it possible that all the sadness she'd suffered since her mother's death had been leading her here?

Was God truly working in her life, as Emma suggested?

Mary lay back into the down of the soft quilt and stared through the open window at the starry sky, alive with the sound of night creatures. Oh, how she wished her dear mother were here to reassure her. As she gazed into the heavens, she thought of her brothers, Ethan and Brody. The same moon shown on them. Stars twinkled above their heads, too. Somehow, the thought made her feel closer. She prayed that God had been as kind to them as He was being to her.

She realized, as time had passed, she was almost considering Ed's abandonment a blessing. Now, sad to say, she didn't miss him at all. It had been almost four weeks and still no word from him. Did he really think Ryzzi Kryzika was a suitable protector?

Did Ed even think?

With a sigh, Mary rose to wash up before undressing for bed. But as her feet touched the floor, she was surprised again by a sudden wave of dizziness.

She leaned back against the bed, waiting for it to pass.

This was so unlike her. She'd been plenty tired before, that was for sure. But the only other time she'd felt faint was when her dad had popped her on the jaw. That had rattled her brains all right. But this was different.

Suddenly, the truth hit her. She had not had her monthly flow since she'd left New York. Not since she'd married Ed. That was over two months ago.

She was with child!

God help her.

eight

Bone weary but unable to sleep, Mary lay in the dark, staring up at the ceiling. If she'd felt angry at Ed before, it was nothing to what she felt now. Anger. Hurt. Despair. Despair worse than any she could ever remember, and she'd had plenty of experience to compare it to.

Without him, what was going to happen to her?

Now that she really needed Ed, the thought of never seeing him again loomed with frightening possibility.

She was probably getting her just reward, she thought miserably, for those fleeting moments when she'd hoped he might never return. Those moments when she'd longed for a good and responsible man.

A man like Magistrate Reed.

Faintly she could hear voices from the kitchen and knew he was still there. Nandi was probably feeding the men.

Now that Mrs. Emma was out of danger, they had nothing more to worry about.

But not Mary. Added trouble was heaped on her head, and she saw even more in her future. If Ed didn't come back, what other man would want her? Without Ed she had no proof that she was even married. A fallen woman, that's what they'd think. Alone, penniless, with a baby to take care of.

What was to become of her?

Oh, how she wished she could sleep. Forget. At least for a time.

And, at last, she did.

❧

"Mary, Mary, we need you!" Reverend Bryant's frantic voice

penetrated the sweet oblivion of sleep.

Mary bolted upright."

"Mary, wake up." She could hear his fist pounding on the paneled door. "It's Emma, something's terribly wrong. It's too soon for the baby—too soon."

"I'll be right there." Mary threw off the quilt and swung her feet to the floor. Dizzy again, she gripped the bedpost, waiting for it to subside, then grabbed her robe.

She found the minister kneeling beside Emma's bed, her hand grasped tightly in his. What a sad tableau. He, still wearing the soiled clothes in which he'd traveled, his distraught, unshaven face hovering close to hers; she, lying beneath the lace coverlet, pale and still.

For an instant, Mary thought her dead, but then Emma's eyelids flickered open. "I'm sorry," she managed before she gasped from another wave of pain. "Oh, Daniel, pray for me."

"I will, my dearest—"

Pray? That made no sense at all. "You must go for the doctor," Mary cried.

"Don't leave me," Emma begged. "Don't leave me, Daniel."

"I won't leave you, darling." He turned to Mary. "Colin will go."

Magistrate Reed was still here?

Mary found him sitting at the cluttered kitchen table, looking almost as distraught as Reverend Bryant.

He lurched to his feet as she entered. "What can I do to help? Tell me what to do."

"You can go after Dr. Lukin."

She had barely finished the sentence before he was out the door.

Mary stood by the window and watched him mount his horse. The animal leaped forward. A less skilled rider would have been thrown, but the magistrate leaned into him, urging the stallion on. She listened to the clap of hooves and tracked the horse and rider until they disappeared into the darkness.

The Bryants were lucky to have such a true and loyal friend as Magistrate Reed. Mary wiped an unbidden tear. And so was she.

Turning back into the kitchen, she drew a pitcher of water, retrieved a glass and bowl from the cupboard, a clean towel from the drawer, and returned to the bedroom.

As she laid what she'd brought on the table beside the bed, Emma managed a wan smile, then shuddered and cried out as another pain beset her.

Reverend Bryant bowed his head over their tightly clasped hands. "Blessed be God, the Father of mercy and the God of all comfort, who comforteth us in all our tribulation—"

Pouring water into the glass, Mary slid onto the other side of the bed beside Emma and slipped her arm around the woman's shoulders. "Try and drink this, dear, it may help," she urged, lifting the glass to Emma's lips.

Valiantly, Emma tried to do as she was asked but fell back from the effort, only to stiffen again, as another pain hurtled through her. "I. . .I'm so. . .much trouble."

After it had passed, Mary stroked her arm, now lying like a dead weight beside her protruding belly. "Just try and relax, the doctor will be here soon."

Emma's body jerked convulsively and again she cried out. The spasms were coming faster.

Mary recognized the pain etched on her dear benefactor's face. She knew the signs. She knew what to do.

She'd seen it all before—when her neighbor had died in childbirth.

Oh, dear God, please don't let that happen to Mrs. Emma.

She wrung out the towel she'd dipped in the bowl of water and gently bathed Emma's brow with the cool, damp cloth, and then her neck and along her arm. Emma seemed to calm briefly, but not for long. Faster and faster the pains came, until Emma seemed oblivious to anything else. Sheathed in sweat, she writhed beneath the rumpled quilt, her sheet-white face contorted, her once-lustrous dark hair lank and tangled on the damp pillow as her neck corded, straining against the paroxysms of pain.

And through it all Reverend Bryant knelt beside her, murmuring a continuous stream of prayer. Then he lifted his eyes and reached for Mary's hand. "Pray with me, Mary."

For an instant she feared he expected her to pray aloud. What was she supposed to say?

But as he took her hand and held it, uncomfortably tight, he began, "Dear Heavenly Father, I beseech you to show mercy for your servant, Emma. Take away this terrible pain and give her peace—" He thanked God for bringing him and Emma together, and as he expressed his deep love and commitment, Mary felt the power of his words coursing from his hand to hers, and into her heart. She could hardly breathe. It was as if all had fallen away, all movement, all sound, all but the prayer from this devoted man who was so very close to his God.

She peeked out from beneath her lowered lashes.

Calm suddenly seemed to have enveloped Emma. Although she was breathing heavily, an expression of peace had transformed her face. Her body seemed to have relaxed.

Had God answered Reverend Bryant's prayer so swiftly? Was the reverend's communication with his Lord that real? That certain? Mary was dumbstruck. The servants had prayed for days to that same God, and so had she. But what they saw of God's mercy had come so slowly. The improvement so gradual. Nothing like this sudden change.

She had heard of Reverend Bryant's miraculous healing. Now she was a witness.

The pains had stopped.

Then she saw it, a red stain seeping into the lace coverlet.

She wrenched her hand from Reverend Bryant's and rolled

back the quilt. Blood soaked the sheet and Emma's gown. The baby lay there. Very small. Very still.

She heard Reverend Bryant gasp.

Mary snatched up the baby. She shook it, slapped its bottom, refusing to believe it was dead.

But the tiny infant did not stir.

Her eyes filmed with tears, she finally gave up. Gently, she wrapped it in a towel and laid it at the foot of the bed.

"I'm so sorry," Emma whispered, looking into her husband's face with the saddest eyes Mary had ever seen.

Tears rolled down his cheeks, and he began to stroke Emma's matted hair. But instead of words of comfort for his grieving wife, he started to pray. Again. For the *baby.*

Consumed by her own sadness for her dear friend, Mary could not believe her ears.

"—and I know you will care for our first-born, until we are called to join him. What a joyous reunion that will be."

Mumbling something about boiling water for the doctor, Mary fled.

She ran down the hall, sobbing.

What kind of a man was this Daniel Bryant? His simple acceptance. His talk of a happy reunion. For their whole lives he and Emma had been laboring in the vineyard of the Lord, and this was the way He repaid them.

Why wasn't Reverend Bryant angry, as she, Mary, was angry at this God she had just begun to trust?

❧

Colin breathed a sigh of relief as he found the spot of light blinking through the trees. Almost there. He urged his horse forward, galloping farther ahead of the doctor's small carriage. It seemed to have taken an hour, but he realized it had only been half that. Dr. Lukin had seemed interminably slow getting dressed. And if Colin hadn't offered to hitch his carriage, they'd probably be there still.

He swung his stallion into the drive, the doctor's buggy clattering behind. Leaping from his mount, he passed the reins to Jalamba, who had run from his quarters to secure the horses.

As he turned, the kitchen door flung open, and in the flood of light, he recognized Mary's silhouette.

Heedless of the doctor, he rushed ahead, across the drive, and up the steps. He took both her hands in his. "Emma—" But he need not finish his question. The answer was written on her tear-streaked face. "Oh, no." His words came out in a guttural moan.

"The baby is gone," she sobbed.

Colin took Mary into his arms. Her head lay against his heart, and he felt his shirt dampened by her tears.

Dr. Lukin crowded past and hurried down the hall.

"And Emma, is she—" Colin was almost afraid to ask. He felt as he had when he was a small boy, waiting for news of his mother.

"Alive. But oh, sir, she is so pale. I'm afraid—" And Mary's slender form shook with renewed sobs.

She released herself from his embrace, wiping her eyes with the back of her hand. "Oh, sir, I am sorry."

Whirling around, she ran to the stove, where a kettle of water boiled. "The doctor will need it." She grabbed an armful of towels and lifted the pot by its handle.

"Let me carry that." Colin stepped forward and tried to take it from her.

But she shook her head and held tight. "No. I must do it," she said, struggling to keep the heavy vessel from tilting. "I need to feel as if I'm of help."

Colin paced the kitchen from one corner to the other and around the table. He saw Mary flying down the hall with an armful of sheets. How did she have the energy? She looked so frail and tired.

A few minutes later she returned. She leaned against the frame of the kitchen door. "The doctor has given Mrs. Emma something to make her sleep. He thinks she'll be fine."

Relieved beyond words, Colin exhaled, feeling his taut muscles begin to relax.

"Just fine." A weary smile barely lifted the corners of Mary's mouth.

She looked so small and forlorn, Colin longed to wipe away the circles of fatigue that smudged her sad brown eyes.

She tightened the sash of her dressing gown and wiggled the toe of a bare foot, giving him a depreciating glance. "I guess you're thinking what a mess I look."

His fingers ached to smooth the tangle of silky cinnamon curls swirling around her shoulders. "That's not what I was thinking."

Not quite meeting his gaze, she said, "I was thinking how blessed the Bryants are to have such a good and faithful friend as you, sir."

Her simple, heartfelt words warmed his heart more than any compliment he could remember. "And more than fortunate to have you. I can't help wondering what might have happened to dear Emma had you not been here. Now, she'll need you more than ever."

Mary sighed deeply. "I'm not so sure, sir, when she finds out that. . .that—" She turned her face away.

Colin walked across the tiled floor to her. "What is it, little one?" When Mary didn't reply, he lifted her chin, forcing her to look into his eyes. "What's troubling you?"

"I'm not sure I'll be so welcome when they find out I'm with child," she whispered.

Colin felt as if he'd just taken a fist in his solar plexus. "You're *what*?"

Mary's shoulders sagged. "You heard right, sir."

"Oh, for heaven's sake, Mary, stop calling me sir. I'm not

some dottering old uncle." He turned violently away. "With child," he muttered, stalking the length of the kitchen. "That's just dandy!"

"It may not be dandy, Magistrate Reed," Mary said, drawing herself up. "But that's the way it is."

"And don't call me Magistrate Reed." He glowered at her.

"What I call you will matter little very soon, since I probably will not be around to call you anything."

"Don't say that," he barked. And was immediately contrite. "Oh, Mary, I'm so sorry. Of all people, you're the last one who deserves my wrath. The last one I'd want to hurt." He moved back to her. "Please forgive me."

"There's nothing to forgive, Mag—"

"Colin. Call me Colin."

She looked at him askance. "Oh, I couldn't possibly. It wouldn't be seemly."

"It wouldn't be seemly to disobey the magistrate," he said, softening his tone. "Friends again?"

"You'll always be my friend. You know that. . .Colin."

"Now, Mary," he said, thoughtfully, "we must deal with your. . .condition. I think it might be better if you didn't mention it to the Bryants just yet. Under the circumstances."

"I'd come to that conclusion myself."

"And as for the Bryants turning you out? Never! I'd stake my reputation on that. But if you would be uncomfortable staying on, I'm certain I can place you elsewhere."

"You won't have to go to all that trouble." Mary looked toward the window. "I'm sure Ed will send for me soon."

🙣

It was almost dawn before Colin started back to his room at the men's club. Only the echo of his stallion's hooves broke the silence. In the grainy light just before the sun squinted over the eastern hills, the world looked as gray and sad as he felt. But as he rode, the crow of a cock, the bark of a dog, offered the promise of a new day.

He sighed. This would be the first morning in four weeks that he wouldn't awaken with Daniel on a nearby bedroll. He realized how much he would miss his friend. He'd even miss the daily devotionals Daniel held for the Christians in his company—not for himself, but for the philosophical discussions they initiated between the two of them. And even though Colin didn't believe a word, he found Daniel's blessings before their meals oddly soothing.

But now, after what he had just witnessed, Colin was finding it harder than ever to understand how an intelligent man like Daniel could believe so completely in a God who, on one hand, could be so cruel as to take away your most cherished possession, and on the other, claim to shower you with a love that would sustain you in the loss. A God who could snatch the very food of your soul and then "lay a table before you."

Colin wouldn't have a friend like that. Let alone a God.

As his mind sorted through the events of the previous day, he thought of Mary and her added burden. His dear sweet Mary. More and more he thought of her as his, while less and less he had a right.

He liked the way her voice sounded when she spoke his name, husky and hesitant. The way her lips formed around the word, lingered on it.

Was this to be his lot? To find the one woman who captivated him and have her forever beyond his reach?

Angry and frustrated, he urged his trotting horse to a gallop.

If it took his last living breath, he would find that black-hearted devil, Ed McKenzie. Drag him back. Make him take responsibility for Mary and her unborn child.

❧

The days of caring for Emma's needs had passed swiftly since Emma's miscarriage. . .too swiftly for Mary to find the right moment to tell Emma about her own baby. Mary sat on the back terrace sipping her second cup of afternoon tea, trying to come up with the right words, when she heard the piano. She hopped up from her chair and ran into the kitchen and down the hall, peeking in Emma's room as she passed. The bed was empty.

Sure enough, there the woman was, in the parlor, only a fortnight since she'd lost her baby. . .against doctor's orders. . . against Daniel's orders. . .*against Mary's orders,* although Mary had very little influence in such matters.

Emma, in a frilly blue wrapper, paused when Mary entered. With a furtive smile, she lifted a finger to her lips in a sign that this was to be their secret, then resumed playing.

If Pastor Daniel were here, his wife would be back in bed. But he had gone to the church a half-hour ago, leaving Mary in charge.

She shook her head at the recalcitrant "child" in her dear friend. Though, what harm, if it lifted Mrs. Emma's spirits? Mary shrugged and moved to stand behind the woman, placing her hands gently on Emma's shoulders as she played.

It was a beautiful, lazy afternoon, clear and sunny. A cool breeze wafted through the parlor window, bringing the promise of autumn while carrying the fragrant perfume of late summer blooms. They mixed pleasantly with the scent of freshly polished furniture.

"What are you playing, Mrs. Emma?"

"A Mozart sonata."

"Mmm." Mary loved when Mrs. Emma played in church, but even more when she played at home. This composition was so elegant, so passionate, almost bringing tears to her eyes. And to think this music had existed hundreds of years and Mary had never been privy to it, not even once, before she'd come to be with the Bryants.

"What Daniel doesn't know won't hurt him," Emma said,

ending with a flourish. She swung around on the piano stool. "I simply had to get out of that room. The walls were beginning to close in on me."

Mary smiled. "It looks to have done you some good. You're glowing." Impulsively, she leaned over, embraced Emma, and gave her a kiss on the cheek.

"Oh, dear girl." Emma hugged her back. "I don't know what I would have done without you through all this." She turned back to the piano.

As she did, Mary noticed Emma's eyes had misted, and a sweet warmth melted Mary's heart.

"Now, you must sing." And Emma began to play "In The Gloaming."

Mary hesitated. Why did that have to be the song Emma chose? The haunting words, the sweet melody that always made her think of Colin. But what didn't? Ever since he'd left ten days ago she could scarcely think of anything else. She'd never forget the expression in his eyes when he'd told her he would be returning to his patrol and would not give up until he found Ed and brought him back. To her and her child.

"Please," Emma begged, beginning the song's introduction again.

Reluctantly, Mary began to sing. "In the gloaming, Oh, my darling, When the lights are dim and low. And the quiet shadows falling softly come and softly go. When the winds are sobbing faintly, with a gentle unknown woe; Will you think of me and love me, as you did once long ago."

When the song came to its end, Emma lowered her hands into her lap and sat, silent. Finally she spoke. "Oh, my dear, sweet Mary. I cannot express how beautiful that was. It made me want to weep."

But the poignant moment was interrupted by the clapping of the front door knocker.

They heard the murmur of voices in the hall, and a moment later Kweela presented Emma with two embossed cards on a small silver tray.

"Oh, it's Sylvia Harcourt, Henry's wife," Emma exclaimed, picking up the cards. "I told you about her, Mary."

"The 'audience' at your musicales."

Emma nodded. "And Grace Ellen Fitzsimmon," she read from the other card. "This must be Sylvia's friend from England. Do invite them in, Kweela, and please ask Nandi to prepare some refreshments."

Barely had Kweela disappeared than two elegantly dressed women swept into the parlor.

"Don't get up, my dear," the shorter of the two commanded, rushing forward.

She reminded Mary of a purple pouty-pigeon in her puce silk day gown, its pleated bodice squeezed in at the waist by a wide matching belt. It must have been the height of fashion because it couldn't have been more unattractive in color or design. But oh, the matching hat. Lacquered feathers and stiff ribbons bounced gloriously atop the wide purple brim.

"It is such a delight to see you, Sylvia." Emma rose, grasping her hands as the woman bestowed a kiss on both cheeks.

"I hope we haven't come too soon after your tragedy, Emma dear."

Mary thought the woman none too worried at the possibility or she wouldn't have included a stranger in the visit.

"Of course not. I'm so happy to see you. If you'll forgive my appearance." Emma smiled ruefully down at the silk dressing gown that Mary thought made her look lovely, and suitably frail.

"I so wanted you to meet my dear, dear friend, Grace Ellen Fitzsimmon, from London, you remember. She and her father are staying with the Norwoods."

Tall and elegant, Grace Ellen Fitzsimmon stood a little

behind, leaning languidly on a pink parasol that matched the rest of her exquisite attire. Mary doubted she'd ever seen a lovelier creature. Clearly, these ladies' outfits were not produced in a New York factory.

The soft, silk fabric of the woman's dress was sprinkled with roses and embellished with a delicate lace. She wore a bonnet trimmed with stiff pink ribbons and silk roses, and long white kid gloves stretched to her elbows.

Any man would be proud to have such a beauty on his arm.

Mary looked down at her own simple pale yellow dress, which up until this moment she'd thought quite fine. Inwardly she sighed, and then was heartened by the thought that even Emma did not possess such fine clothes—yet still had twice the bearing.

The young woman extended her hand. "I'm so happy to finally meet the famous Mrs. Bryant, about whom I've heard such glowing reports." Her pale blue eyes widened with compassion. "Allow me to express my condolences over your loss."

"Thank you," Emma replied quietly. "We don't always know the Lord's plan for us. But He does have one. Daniel and I are confident of that. And now," she turned, "may I introduce *my* house guest, Mary McKenzie." Emma bestowed an encouraging smile. "Mary has indeed been a blessing during this time."

Mary dipped her head. "I am very pleased to meet you," she enunciated in the proper way that Emma had taught her.

"And now, you must all sit down. Our cook is preparing refreshments, which should be ready any minute."

How gracious and at ease Mrs. Emma seemed; not intimidated at all by these wealthy ladies, although she'd once confessed to Mary that she was rather shy.

"It's simply been a whirlwind of social activities and invitations since Grace Ellen arrived, hasn't it?" Mrs. Harcourt cast a smile at her friend as she settled onto the couch. "And why not," she gushed, "with such a beautiful, charming—to say nothing of well-connected—young lady?"

Miss Fitzsimmon smiled demurely.

"She's related to a niece by marriage of the Third Earl of Devon, you know," Mrs. Harcourt added. "And my dear, she has a singing voice that could charm the wings off angels."

"How lovely! Mary, too, has a wonderful voice," Emma inserted, trying to draw Mary into the conversation.

"Oh, were you the one singing when we arrived?" Grace Ellen asked pleasantly.

Mary nodded.

"Very nice." Mrs. Harcourt dismissed that topic with a brief smile and got to what Mary surmised was the real reason for their visit. "When do you suppose you will be up to resuming our little musicales?" She glanced at her friend. "Now that Colin's back."

Magistrate Reed was back? Mary's heart leaped at the unexpected news.

"We've quite literally been waiting for his return with bated breath. In my humble opinion," Mrs. Harcourt giggled, "Colin is the most eligible bachelor in Johannesburg. I take that back. In Transvaal—perhaps the whole of South Africa."

All but Mary joined in the laughter.

"—even the entire British Empire."

They all laughed again.

Mrs. Harcourt leaned forward. "In fact," she said, her tone conspiratorial, "I think Colin has his eye on Grace Ellen. Now wouldn't that be a match!"

nine

Mary stood quietly in the archway of the parlor as Emma and the two ladies lingered in the entry over their good-byes.

"We'll look forward to our Thursday musicale, then," Mrs. Harcourt said. "I hope Daniel won't put up too much of a fuss." At the bottom step, she turned. "And, of course, your charming house guest simply must join us. With her lovely contralto, she and Grace Ellen could perform a duet. Grace Ellen is a trained soprano."

"I think that's a wonderful idea," Emma said from where she stood on the front stoop. "We'll see you then on Thursday at seven."

Mary stood speechless behind her as Emma waved at her departing guests.

Sing with the English lady? One who is a trained soprano?

The rich ladies waved back and smiled as they were assisted into their carriage by a smartly dressed black driver.

"How could you, Mrs. Emma?" Mary cried before Emma could even shut the door. "How could you agree to have me sing in front of those ladies? Every word that comes out of their mouths is so perfectly spoken, and Miss Fitzsimmon's accent is so. . .so refined. Why I—"

Emma drew her back into the parlor. "Come and sit down, Mary. I think we need to talk."

Mary sighed in despair as she seated herself on the settee next to her patron. She was sure that Mrs. Emma had come to her senses and realized the folly of it, too. Mary just wasn't yet educated enough for "polite society." And possibly never would be.

Emma took both Mary's hands in hers. "My dear child, you must stop thinking of yourself as less worthy merely because you didn't have certain advantages when you were young. If our Heavenly Father sees all His earthly children as worthy of entering His grandest of heavens, that's sufficient for the Bryants. And as for your singing, you must trust me, dear. I would not expect you to do this if I didn't think you were ready. I have the utmost confidence in your ability." She gave Mary an encouraging smile. "In all ways, you have proven to have such a quick mind. And a lovely, sensitive soul."

"But Mrs. Emma—"

"No buts about it."

"Believe me, Mrs. Emma, I'm really not all that worthy of your confidence. And I'm *certainly* not worthy of this grandest of heavens you talk about."

"Why nonsense, dear. You think I don't know the heart of a Christian when I see one?" She gave Mary a droll smile. "And by now I should be an expert!" Patting Mary's hand, she said, "You've been my true companion and friend these past weeks, praying with me in my dark hours. I don't know what I would have done without you. I am deeply in your debt."

Mary hung her head. "I wish you wouldn't keep saying such nice things about me. I'm not that deserving. Besides, I'm not at all sure that God hears my prayers. And I wouldn't blame Him if He didn't." Mary wrung her hands. "I may be your true friend, Mrs. Emma, but I haven't been an honest one."

Emma tilted her head, and a frown line formed between her brows. "What is it, dear?"

"I'm. . .I'm—" She struggled to get out the words, and then they came all in a rush. "I'm with child."

Emma flinched.

"There! Now you know." Fighting back tears, Mary rose. "How can I stay here and be a living reminder of what happened to you? I am so sorry. Truly I am." She took a deep breath. "It won't take me long to pack."

"Pack? Whatever for?" Emma rose to her feet. "Is there something you left out? Something more you haven't told me?"

"More? Isn't that enough?" Mary looked incredulous. "Especially given your fragile state."

"My fragile state. Posh! Does that mean I must henceforth banish all mothers-to-be?" Emma took Mary's hand again. "Don't you see, my dear, every new life is a gift from God. And as painful as my loss has been, this child you are carrying is God's gift. To *all* of us." She threw her arms around Mary. "You've given us something special to look forward to."

Mary didn't know what to say. She hardly knew what to feel. All she knew was that this saintly woman had made her see the baby, growing inside her, as a blessing instead of a burden.

Mary suddenly realized that for the first time in her life, she would have something precious she could call her own. A baby. Her baby.

"It's my guess," Emma said, "that if he hasn't already, Colin will soon find your Edward. Everything will turn out as it should in the end. You'll see."

Mary gave her a wan, uncertain smile.

"We have our Heavenly Father's word on it."

"You really believe that."

Emma looked her straight in the eye with an unflinching gaze. "You can count on it."

Still, Mary wondered.

How could Mrs. Emma, of all people, be so sure?

❧

The grandfather clock in the hall struck the hour and a quarter. Their guests would be arriving in fifteen minutes.

Mary's stomach fluttered. In the hall mirror she stared at the reflection of a young woman she hardly recognized. Her thick auburn hair was parted in the middle, waved deep on either side of her brow and swept up in a tumble of curls at her crown, the way Mrs. Emma had fashioned it. Into it she had pinned a silk rose that matched Mary's silvery, pink gown.

Mary tucked a recalcitrant curl back into the clustered curls.

What if the pins came loose and the whole thing fell down in the middle of the musicale? Oh, how had she let herself be talked into this?

Nervously she tugged at the frilled-lace, high-boned collar that had scratched a red spot on her neck. At least Mrs. Emma hadn't made her wear one of those tight corsets that gave ladies the vapors.

Thank you, Lord, for small blessings.

Daniel, his own collar white as chalk and starched as stiff, came down the hall and paused. His gentle smile reflected back at her in the mirror. "You look beautiful, Mary."

"Oh, Pastor Daniel, how can I believe you? You'd tell me that if I looked like a scullery maid."

"Scullery maid? Grand lady is much more like it." His smile broadened, and he recited, " 'What's in a name? That which we call a rose, by any other name would smell as sweet.' "

Mary frowned.

"William Shakespeare. An English poet and playwright. Emma will teach you about him in due time, my dear." He gave her arm a pat.

Mary swung around as Emma swept out of the bedroom, elegant and blooming in an ivory silk gown that complimented the luster of her hair. Pale smudges beneath her large dark eyes seemed to be the only vestiges left of her delicate condition.

"Oh, Mrs. Emma. Tell me the truth. Please. Do I really look presentable?"

With knitted brow, Emma tilted her head first to one side,

then the other, scrutinizing Mary with mock consideration. "In my opinion," she said, her voice *very* serious, "any addition to your loveliness would be redundant and excessive ostentation."

"Whatever that means," Mary giggled.

"But you get my point." Emma gave her a hug.

"Thank you for letting me wear this." Mary touched the cameo at her throat.

"No one will recognize it as mine, so you don't have to tell." She smiled fondly at her husband. "I always wear the one Daniel gave me on our wedding day."

Oh, to have a marriage like theirs. So full of trust and shared purpose and, most of all, a genuine unselfish love for one another.

"Thank you both. I'll try to remember everything you taught me, Mrs. Emma, and not embarrass you."

"Just relax." Daniel smiled encouragement and moved down the hall. "Be the lovely lady you are, my dear child, and you'll have nothing to fear."

Relax.

Men had no idea. She would be judged in the same unforgiving light as that elegant English lady. Even her singing. By everybody. By Magistrate Reed. She doubted she could bring herself to call him Colin. Especially in front of all those strangers.

A cryptic note to the Bryants was all she'd heard of him since he'd returned from the north. And nothing was mentioned about Ed.

Surely, by now, Colin had located him.

Perhaps Ed had sent a message with orders for her to join him. That possibility only added to her anxiety.

She jumped at the sound of the carriage wheels clattering to a stop in front. But then she felt the comfort of Emma's arm around her as her friend led her into the parlor.

"Take a few deep breaths, my dear. This is not the hangman's noose we're awaiting. Just a friendly visit with friends."

Mary could hear the front door open, Pastor Daniel's welcome, the women's gay chatter, the men's robust greetings. . . Colin's voice.

She and Emma turned as the ladies entered.

Mary's throat tightened.

Grace Ellen Fitzsimmon was more breathtaking than the afternoon they'd met. The jonquil silk dress brought out the amazing blue of her eyes, its scooped neck accentuating the pale, graceful line of her throat. The trim of lavender silk roses emphasized her full bosom and the matching sash, her tiny waist.

It was the height of fashion, and it undoubtedly cost a king's ransom.

She glanced down at her own simple frock and felt like a child.

Mrs. Harcourt's pale orange ensemble was just as fashionable, but beside her tall, stately friend, she seemed an overripe caricature of a plump pumpkin.

Daniel ushered in a short, bandy-legged gentleman lugging a cello case as round as he. He had a pleasant freckled face and a fringe of red hair. He could only be Mrs. Harcourt's husband. Mary suppressed a smile. Two round pumpkins in a patch.

Then her breath caught.

Bringing up the rear, violin case in hand, was Magistrate Reed. . .Colin looking taller and even more magnificent than she remembered.

The cut of his expensively tailored suit made his shoulders seem broad enough to fill the entry, and his skin looked like burnished bronze against his white, starched collar. His helmet of curly dark hair was tamed, save for one eccentric lock that hung rakishly over his right brow.

And his smile. Oh, his smile. It lit into the darkest corners.

Mrs. Harcourt was right. He and Grace Ellen Fitzsimmon would, indeed, make a handsome couple.

And that's as it should be. So why this sudden stab of sadness?

But that smile, that brilliant, dashing smile was turned, not on Miss Fitzsimmon, but on Mary as he strode into the room.

"Colin, dear. . ." Miss Fitzsimmon stepped out of the shadows—for the whole room seemed to darken in his dazzle—and snagged his arm. "Colin, dear, have you met the Bryants' house guest, Mary McKinney?"

"*McKenzie.* Mary McKenzie," Colin corrected, holding Mary in his warm gaze. "Indeed I have. We're old friends. In fact, it was I who introduced her to the Bryants'."

Oh, good heavens. He wasn't going to tell Grace Ellen how they'd met, was he?

"You look lovely this evening, Mary," he said.

Weak with relief, Mary felt a flush creep up her cheeks.

"I understand you and Grace Ellen are going to sing for us this evening." He turned to the woman on his arm.

Mrs. Harcourt, who had joined them, gave Mary a pleasant smile. "You have a sweet voice, Mary. It should accompany Grace Ellen's nicely."

Condemned with faint praise. "Thank you, Mrs. Harcourt."

"We heard Mary the other afternoon when we came to visit Emma," the woman said to Colin. "Her contralto will blend well with our Grace Ellen's divine soprano." The little woman clasped her hands to her bosom. "Wait until you hear her. I declare, Colin, Grace Ellen has the voice of an angel."

Mary's stomach turned to quivering jelly. She feared she might throw up. Blending her nice voice with a soprano of pure perfection.

She seriously wondered if she'd make it through the evening.

*

As the clock chimed nine times, the last strains of "I Dream of Jeanne" ended to the enthusiastic applause of the gathered friends.

Flushed with delight at how well the evening was going, Mary dipped her head shyly in response, while Grace Ellen Fitzsimmon gave a sweeping curtsy in Magistrate Reed's direction.

Whether Mary wanted to admit it or not, she had begun to suspect it was she, Mary, who might be the reason for the woman's clinging possessiveness of the magistrate.

She could hardly believe it. For certain, she had given Grace Ellen no reason. And there was no doubt Magistrate Reed had treated Mary with no more gentlemanly consideration than he always treated her—than he treated all the ladies. That this stunningly beautiful, high-born, English woman should be jealous of a nobody like herself—well, it was just unbelievable. A *married* nobody, at that. If Grace Ellen only knew. And Mary was taking a wicked delight in not being the one to tell her.

Emma swiveled around on the piano stool. "Now, everyone, I think it's time for an intermission." As she rose to lead them into the dining room for refreshments, a wild scream pierced through the open French doors.

Grace Ellen let out a squeal, nearly as shrill, and ran into the protective custody of Colin's arms.

"Just some lonely night hunter expressing his appreciation for your singing," he laughed.

"Odd. Sounded like a leopard." Henry raised his brows. "Not many left this far south. I'll wager half the men in Johannesburg are reaching for their hunting rifles as we speak. Poor beast."

"Poor Emma. You must be in a constant fear, living so close to the wild." Grace Ellen nestled deeper into Colin's embrace, shivering with fear.

It did seem a little excessive.

"Speaking of wild, Daniel," Colin said, discreetly removing his arm from around the woman's shoulders, "one of these days you're going to have to explain how Noah, in your Bible, managed to convince all those animals to get along in that one little boat. He must have been some zoo keeper."

"I'd be delighted to discuss it at length," Daniel offered. "When did you have in mind?"

Henry guffawed. "You asked for it, Colin."

"You're welcome to join us, Henry." Daniel shifted his falsely benign smile to Henry, and everyone laughed.

Everyone but Mary.

Was it possible that an educated man like Colin was not familiar with the significance of Noah and the ark? Why, that was one of the first stories Emma had her read.

He must be jesting.

She added her small laugh to the rest.

As she watched them all troop out of the parlor, two by two, Grace Ellen clinging to Colin's arm, Mary felt like odd-man-out. If Ed were here she'd have her own partner to accompany her.

And feel even more at odds.

She couldn't imagine an uneducated braggart like Ed ever fitting in with these refined people.

Braggart?

When had she started thinking of her husband in such an unflattering light? She turned toward the French doors. Right now fresh air attracted her far more than food anyway.

As she stood on the verandah, she peered into the darkness toward the north. Ed was out there somewhere, and someday he would return for her. Then evenings like this would be gone forever. Ed's world was saloons and card rooms. She sighed. But he was the man she'd married. And the father of this precious new life inside her. She placed a hand on her, as yet, flat belly. Maybe when Ed learned about the baby he'd change. Maybe he'd be willing to make a proper home for them. Go to church.

Maybe. Maybe. Maybe.

Grace Ellen's trilling, high-pitched laughter cut through Mary's thoughts. It grated on her nerves more than any old wildcat's scream.

By now, the "clinging vine" probably had both of her beautiful arms wrapped around Magistrate Reed's neck.

ten

Tricky business, Colin thought, trying not to show his irritation as strawberry punch sloshed from his cup onto the front of his vest.

Using his arm as a swivel base, Grace Ellen turned from him to Sylvia and back, exchanging the latest gossip. As if it interested him in the least.

"Carolyn Wilkins knows for a fact that Reggie Carson is keeping company with the daughter of one of his foremen. A Boer. Can you imagine?"

"A Boer? *Really?*" From Sylvia's shocked expression, one would almost have expected they'd found a dead body pinned to the wall. "Did you hear that, Henry?" She turned back to Grace Ellen. "I hope he doesn't expect us to take her into our circle."

In warning, Colin cleared his throat, and Sylvia shot a guilty look at Daniel.

"I'm sorry, Daniel. They're not all of them bad," Sylvia hastened to acknowledge. "But you must admit, they are a different breed. Most of them are uneducated farmer types, speaking some aberrant version of German."

Colin saw Daniel's expression stiffen and wondered what precisely chosen words of admonishment would follow. And not necessarily all that tactful. Americans, especially those from their northern states, were particularly sensitive about that "all men are created equal sort of thing," after fighting a civil war to free their own slaves.

"Dr. Shultz, my German instructor, is a Boer. And highly educated," Emma mused. "So I guess one never knows." She shrugged prettily. "Bye the bye, Sylvia, I just received some photographs of mother and my sister Margaret that I've been wanting to show you. Do come along, too, Grace Ellen."

Colin felt as if a hundred-and-fifteen-pound weight—or thereabout—had been removed as Emma looped her arm through Grace Ellen's, drawing her toward the archway leading out of the dining room.

"You know how anxious I am to get Margie over for a visit, Sylvia," she continued, as the three ladies strolled out of the room.

Confrontation skillfully defused. Chalk one up for Emma.

Colin knew his friend well, and although Daniel was supremely tactful as a rule, there were some issues that set his rhetoric afire. And justice for all was one of them.

Putting down his libation, Colin attempted to brush out the wrinkles Grace Ellen's clutch had ironed into his sleeve. The woman had a grip of steel. He shook his head and ladled punch into a fresh cup. "Perhaps Mary would like something to drink."

"Good idea," Daniel said.

Henry swallowed one bonbon while reaching for another. "She certainly has a strong, rich contralto for such a small, little person," he observed, popping a third into his mouth. "Quite a surprise."

More of a surprise than you know, my friend, Colin thought, strolling out into the starlit darkness.

A shaft of light from the parlor bathed Mary in an amber glow, tinting the tips of her auburn curls with gold.

Colin paused, enchanted.

Perhaps some would consider Grace Ellen the more beautiful. But it was Mary's quiet strength, so reminiscent of his mother, that called to Colin and was so restful to his soul.

As he moved toward her, she turned. "Oh, it's you, Magis. . . Colin." A genuine smile lit her face as she accepted the proffered cup. "Thank you. You are most kind."

"The night cries don't frighten you, I see."

"I much prefer these night cries to them—those of New York."

"Or downtown Johannesburg," he murmured.

Mary's newly schooled words held not a trace of her New York accent. Emma had done a wonderful job, and in less than two months.

He had certainly brought Mary to the right place. Had he taken her to the Harcourts, no doubt by now all the spirit would have been sucked out of her. Sylvia would have treated her like a servant or, at best, snubbed her like the unfortunate Boer girl Reggie Carson was in love with.

Yet, here Mary was, hobnobbing with Sylvia and her English crony, with no one the wiser.

He couldn't help but smile.

Mary tilted her head. "What is so funny?"

He realized he'd been staring. "It's just that. . .I'd hoped to get you alone—I mean—" She was doing it again. How could this sweet, simple girl turn a sophisticated man-of-the-world like himself—leastways that's how he liked to think of himself—into a bowl of mush? "What I mean to say is, I wanted to speak to you privately. About your husband."

Mary's eyes widened. "You have spoken with him. Where is he? When—"

Colin placed a stilling finger on her lips. "Unfortunately, no. I've found no trace. I'm wondering if he might be using an assumed name? Can you think of any reason he'd want to do that?"

He could see her withdraw, wounded by his implication.

"Are you saying he'd want to escape from me so much he'd change his name? I'm sure I never gave him no—any reason to do such a thing."

"I'm sorry, Mary, but I have to ask these questions if we're going to find him. It seems his name and the description you've given just aren't enough. Is there anything you might have overlooked—a scar, a particular habit or mannerism?"

Mary looked thoughtful. "Well, there is one thing. He had this medallion that he was especially proud of. I don't know where he got it. He said it was worth a lot of money—"

"Yes?"

"He used to flip it. You know, when he was standing around, talking, or when he was nervous. It was really distracting." She looked up hopefully at Colin. "Is that the kind of thing you're talking about?"

"Exactly. And if anything else comes to mind, no matter how insignificant it might seem, you must let me know."

"I'll try to think of more, but—"

As far as Colin was concerned, that was enough talk of Ed for now. "Are you feeling better?" he asked.

"Oh, yes."

"No more dizziness?"

She shook her head.

Now for the most pressing topic. "Do you still want me to find you another place? I'm afraid I'll be hard pressed to—"

His voice stilled as she placed her small hand on his, then to his disappointment, withdrew it. "It won't be necessary. I told Emma about the baby. She insisted that I stay." Mary's brown eyes softened to a warm glow. "She called it God's blessing, come to ease their pain. Can you believe it?"

"They are amazing people," Colin agreed. "They manage to turn everything in their lives into something good from their God."

For an instant her glowing eyes sparked bright. "Yes. They do have the most remarkable faith."

"And you, sweet Mary," he said, longing to reach for her hand again, "are the most remarkable, bravest of young ladies."

"Oh, there you two are." Grace Ellen's practiced lilt shattered the moment. Silhouetted by the parlor lights, she swooped down on them.

Colin scarcely managed to keep his groan silent.

"I do believe we're about to begin again," she said, snagging that same arm she'd overused before, crushing the fabric and Colin's hope for more time alone with Mary.

He shot Mary a beleaguered look. Suddenly he realized how important it was to him that she understand.

Grace Ellen Fitzsimmon was not his kind of woman.

❧

Daniel closed the door behind their departing guests. "Well, dear girl, your debut was a great success. Didn't I tell you?"

Mary's answering grin felt broad enough to crack.

"Perhaps we could arrange for our Mary and Grace Ellen to sing a duet in church one Sunday. What do you think, Emma?"

"I think that's a superb idea. What a clever man you are." Emma tweaked her husband's cheek as the three moved back into the parlor.

Mary stood in the archway. "Don't you think I should be consulted first?"

"Of course you should, Mary," Daniel replied as the pair of expectant faces turned in her direction.

"Yes. Yes. Yes," she sang up the scale, twirling toward them and ending with a deep curtsy. "Yes."

Emma and Daniel leaned against each other, laughing and applauding.

"Well, aren't you full of vim and vinegar at this late hour?" Emma said, sinking down into the nearest chair. "I think it was an especially lovely evening, Daniel, don't you?"

"Except for—"

"I know what you're going to say. But basically Sylvia's a decent sort, and Colin and Henry are such close friends."

"I suppose it isn't fair to blame Henry for his wife's prejudices," Daniel grumbled. "We'll just have to pray that the good Lord will remove her blinders."

Standing in front of the fireplace screen, hands behind her back, Mary had a sudden and unpleasant thought. "Col—Magistrate Reed has always seemed so prudent about mentioning the circumstance of our first meeting. I do hope he didn't tell his friend Mr. Harcourt about it. I would be so embarrassed."

"If he did," Daniel said, resting his hand on Emma's shoulder, "I can assure you it would be in the strictest confidence and would go no further. Henry may have his weaknesses, as we all do, but he's an honorable man."

"Don't worry, dear," Emma interjected, "Colin's concern for your well-being is quite genuine. I know that for certain."

"He's given me no reason to doubt that. But still it helps to have your reassurance." Mary walked over to Emma and gave her a kiss on the cheek, and then one for Pastor Daniel. Under the arch, she turned. "Thank you for a wonderful evening."

"Thank you for helping make it so, dear. Good night." Emma's voice followed her down the hall.

But when Mary heard Pastor Daniel mention Colin's name, she paused.

"Colin has so many admirable qualities, it grieves me he will not accept the one true God. He lumps the relationship we have with our Heavenly Father in with all those superstitious fantasies of the natives."

Mary didn't want to hear any more. She slipped into her bedroom and sagged against the door.

She understood Colin's doubts; she'd had them herself. But how could anyone know the Bryants and not see God reflected in their lives? She'd even come to understand what Pastor Daniel meant when he'd prayed for their lost baby and for their joyous reunion in heaven. In the Bryants, she'd witnessed an inner strength and love of which she wanted a share.

Oh, if she'd only known them before she married Ed.

No! She must not think that way. Already she was doubting God's purpose.

But there was one thing, yet, she knew she must do. Once and for all she must confess the sin that had been plaguing her.

She slipped onto her knees beside her bed and bowed her head over her folded hands.

"Forgive me, Lord. Although I've never wanted to admit it, I covet Colin Reed. I have wanted him for my husband so much that I wished Ed would never come back. I am no better than David when he coveted Uriah's wife. It is the same sin. From now on, I will pray only for Ed's safe return. And his soul. . .and Colin's.

"Oh, dear Lord, please, I beg You, give me the strength not to long for more."

⁂

"It's been a delightful evening," Colin said, stepping down from the carriage and breathing a deep and relieved sigh. At last he was rid of Grace Ellen's grasping fingers. He now fully understood why such a beautiful woman was not married. Too many tentacles.

She leaned out the carriage window. "When will we see you again, Colin?"

"I'm afraid not for some time." He never thought he'd be glad for the continuing unrest in the northern mines. "I'll be leaving for the Murchison District day after tomorrow. No telling how long I'll be gone."

"When father said we were coming to Africa, I was frightened we might be overrun by Zulus or some other native savages." Grace Ellen shuddered. "But knowing there are men as brave and strong as you to protect us, I'll not have another moment's distress."

"I appreciate your confidence." Colin felt like laughing. If anyone needed protection, it was the poor Zulus and the other tribes being exploited by the mine owners. . .and, he himself. From Grace Ellen.

Colin shifted his attention to Henry. "If you ladies can spare him for a moment, I have a bit of business to discuss with Henry."

"Of course," Sylvia said, moving aside as her husband clambered out of the cab and followed Colin up the steps of the gentleman's club where he resided.

At the door, Colin turned, glowering at Henry. "I can't handle this anymore."

"What, old chap? Something you need me to do at the bank?"

"No! It's that Fitzsimmon woman. Until she is otherwise occupied, I cannot visit your home or attend any function where she might be present. And," he said, trying to tone down his harried inflections, "I shall expect you to keep me abreast of her movements that I may avoid her."

"You amaze me, old boy," his friend huffed. "The woman is gorgeous. And she certainly makes no secret of wanting to fully express just how much she admires you. If you get my drift." Henry gave him a knowing grin.

"I've been a hunter much too long to let myself fall prey to some grasping huntress."

"So, I was right. You *were* doing a bit of hunting yourself this evening."

Colin felt the stab of his friend's elbow in his ribs.

"I guess there's no accounting for taste." Henry shrugged. "A mere daisy instead of the rose. But if it's the quiet American you prefer, so be it."

"Ha!" Colin gave a sharp laugh. "Quiet? You don't remember who she is, do you?"

"She did look familiar, but I couldn't quite place her."

"She's the one in the telescope. The one fighting off the masher."

"You mean the little—" Henry frowned, "—sparrow? Or

was it wren? The one you deserted us to go and save? You do know I got the dickens about that." The pudgy man sighed. "Well, if she's what you want. . . Sylvia will be disappointed. She had her heart set on matching you with Grace Ellen. But since that's not to be, I suppose my dear wife will just have to switch her energies to Miss McKenzie."

"I think not." Colin thrust his hands into his trouser pockets. "You see, *Miss* McKenzie is *Mrs.* McKenzie."

"You rogue!" Henry exploded.

The desk clerk looked up from his records.

Henry lowered his voice. "I never would have thought it of you."

"Be serious, Henry."

Sobering, Henry lifted his hand to Colin's shoulder. "Do you think you're being wise, old friend? You and your Mrs. McKenzie."

"She's not *my* Mrs. McKenzie," Colin retorted, brushing aside Henry's hand. "I'm merely trying to locate her husband for her."

Henry's eyes reflected his skepticism. "You keep telling yourself that, old chap. But I saw the looks you two exchanged." He pushed open the double glass door. "And so did Grace Ellen. Perhaps it's for the best that you're leaving for the backcountry again. Have a safe trip."

Disturbed by Henry's words more than he wished to admit, Colin watched until his friend reached his carriage. Then he did an about-face. He strode through the nearly empty lobby, up the stairs, and down the long quiet hall to his room. Unlocking the door, he entered the sterile but well-furnished suite.

Without turning on the light, he removed his jacket, dropped it on a chair, and threw himself onto the leather couch.

What was he going to do? If his feelings were that obvious to his often obtuse friend, they would soon be clear to the whole world. He closed his eyes, picturing Mary that first day when she'd come into his office, flushed and disheveled, but so brave and forthright and determined.

I think I loved her even then.

He smiled, remembering how beautiful she'd looked this evening, her practiced diction, her rich, vibrant singing voice. What a surprise that had been.

Emma had not changed Mary. Emma had nurtured and brought out what was already there.

Mary was a woman he knew he could trust with any secret. He could see himself wanting to come home to her, sharing his day, hearing about hers, listening. . .loving—

He groaned and dropped his head into his hands. He had to stop fooling himself, pretending she wasn't married. He may have deluded himself into thinking, *hoping* she'd lied, but Mary would never lie about something that important.

Not only is she married, she's carrying her husband's child.

God in Heaven, why couldn't it have been mine? Why?

It could. If—

His heart hammered. He lunged to his feet, stunned by the direction his thoughts had taken. Just one evening with Mary McKenzie was enough to have him harboring murderous thoughts.

He wouldn't wait until the day after, he'd leave tomorrow. He'd set up a substation in the north. Stay there until he'd gotten the woman out of his system. Once and for all.

eleven

September 1905

Today! She would be baptized today.

Mary's heart was full of unbounded joy and love—so full, there was hardly room to breathe—and gratitude, for all the blessings God had already showered on her, not the least of which were the Bryants.

It was very unusual to be baptized so close to one's time of delivery. She knew that. But once she'd made up her mind, she'd just had to do it. No matter what. No matter she would look like a beached whale in her white shift. She giggled. Anyway, what did God care how she looked? Certainly Pastor Daniel and Mrs. Emma, and Kweela and Nandi and Jalamba didn't care. And they were the only ones who were going to be there.

She looked out her bedroom window, remembering the first day she had come here.

She remembered unpacking her meager belongings, then joining the Bryants and Magistrate Reed for afternoon refreshments. Grapes had hung from the vine winding through the trellis that canopied the verandah, a scented breeze ruffling their leaves. She remembered the frosted glasses of lemonade and the sweets and sandwiches that Magistrate Reed had insisted she eat. How kind and welcoming they had all been, doing their best from the very start to make her feel at home.

She tried not to think of Colin, except in her prayers. She hadn't seen him in six months.

Just as well.

As for Ed, almost eight months had gone by, and she'd heard not a single word—not one—since he'd left her the note, the measly two pounds, and Ryzzi Kryzika as her protector. She'd encountered Ryzzi only once in these past months, downtown, when she and Mrs. Emma were coming out of the dry goods store. Mary had turned her face away, but heard his mumbled epithets as she passed.

"Mary, dear—"

She turned at the sound of Emma's motherly voice beyond her bedroom door. "I'm almost ready," she answered, then at the sharp kick inside her, amended, "*we're* almost ready."

"Jalamba's hitching the carriage. We'll be leaving in about five minutes."

Mary folded her hands over her protruding belly as she stood by the window surveying the sunny yellow room—the four-poster bed with the embroidered coverlet, the chest of polished mahogany. She leaned against the chair by the window that Mrs. Emma had mused was a lovely spot to read. Mary smiled. And now she could!

Her fingers played across a letter lying on the table next to it. It was from her brothers, Brody and Ethan in California, by way of Ruthie, her best friend in New York. Now she not only could read their letter, but answer it.

Next time I write, you will be uncles.

Oh, how she longed to see them. She wondered if she ever would again. If only they were here now. On this special day.

But they are. In my thoughts and in my heart. Always.

It was almost time to go.

Mary slipped into the long-sleeved white cotton shift she'd made for her baptism and hurried over to the dresser. As she ran the brush through her tangle of curls, she glanced into the mirror.

Amazing.

How could she look the same and yet feel so different?

She folded a towel and the dress she would change into after the baptism and placed them in her small valise, then snapped it shut.

At the door she turned for one last look.

The next time she entered this room she would be a new person, reborn in the love of God.

&

"What a glorious warm spring day," Emma extolled. "Absolutely perfect for our purpose." She and Nandi sat in the seat, facing Kweela and Mary. Perched up next to Jalamba on the driver's bench, Daniel began to sing in a lusty baritone, "Shall we gather at the river—" and the rest of the hearty little band joined in.

A group of black folks waved from a nearby shanty, and farther down the road, a white boy on a bicycle tipped his cap.

It seemed as if everyone in the whole world was celebrating this auspicious event. Whether they knew it or not.

Mary's heart quickened as they approached the last bend in the road before they reached the river.

In the distance they heard singing of a different measure. It began as a continuous but melodious hum and, as it moved closer, grew in volume.

Over the crest of the hill they came toward them, a hundredfold or more, their dusky bodies materializing, as if by magic, out of the swirling dust. The women in their orange patterned tunics tied at one shoulder; the men, bare-chested, the same bright cloth secured at their waists by animal pelts.

Mary had never seen, nor could she have imagined, such a sight, as the people filled the road and spread down toward the river.

Jalamba reined in the horses.

"*Ukutulahakubekuwe,*" Daniel shouted. "Peace be with you."

"Who are they?" Mary asked Emma as she craned her neck to see around the front of the carriage.

"Zulus, from the way they're dressed," Emma answered, leaning out to get a better look.

Daniel hopped down from his seat as a small group of natives separated themselves from the rest. In the front stood a large, imposing man, a little older than Pastor Daniel, and beside him, a woman holding a sleeping child.

"Umfundici," the man cried out as Daniel approached.

"That's what the Zulus call Daniel," Emma whispered to Mary.

As the group circled him, a third man seemed to be acting as interpreter. Behind them the singing never stopped, but flowed on, rising and falling, swelling louder then softer, in what seemed one continuous, extended breath.

After a number of minutes Daniel returned, his face registering an expression of deep concern. "It's Prince Buthelezi," he said quietly. "His baby is in a coma."

Nandi frowned. "The baby has got 'the sleep of the dead'."

"Encephalitis?" Emma whispered.

Daniel nodded.

Nandi shook her head sadly. "There is no hope."

"There's always hope, Nandi," Daniel said sharply. "Trust and it shall be given unto thee. Ask, and ye shall receive. Have you forgotten?"

Rebuked, Nandi's heavy-jowled face fell.

At once he said, "I'm sorry, dear friend, I spoke too harshly. Perhaps to bolster my own courage." He touched her hand. "All we can do is ask. The Lord will give us His answer."

Tears stung Mary's lids as she folded her arms protectively over her own unborn child. Now that she was about to become a mother herself, she more fully understood the pain of losing a child. Emma's pain.

"They were on their way to me," Daniel said.

Emma smiled gently. "How providential. They need go no farther."

He grasped her hand. "Oh, dear, Emma, pray that I can be a conduit for God's mercy." With that, he turned and walked toward the river's edge, the people following.

A silence fell over the crowd.

Emma and Nandi stepped down from the carriage. Hands linked, they stood on the grass bank.

Jalamba bowed his head.

Kweela sat, her hands clasped, swaying forward and back, whispering her own affirmation of faith. "Thank you Jesus, thank you Jesus—"

Breath suspended, Mary clutched the side of the carriage, her eyes glued on Pastor Daniel as he placed his hand on the baby's tiny head and began to pray.

No bird sang. No breeze caressed the tufted grass. Even the river seemed to pause. Expectant. Waiting.

A murmur spread through the crowd.

Emma and Nandi were on tiptoes, straining to see. Mary stood up in the carriage to get a better view.

Beside her Kweela, rigid, silent, stared at the baby. "It moved," she whispered.

"The baby moved," breathed Mary, then cried out as she scrambled from the carriage.

The baby's mother began to cry and laugh as she hugged the infant close.

Prince Buthelezi stood still and silent; then, with a mighty shout, wrestled his son from its mother's arms and lifted him high above his head, turning slowly, so that all his people could witness the miracle.

A great cheer rose up.

Tears streamed down Mary's cheeks and mingled with Kweela's and Emma's and Nandi's as they embraced.

The air was charged. The crowd went wild.

Then they began to sing. A joyous song that started by the river and spread across the valley, until the highest branches of the baobab trembled and the stones beneath the waters shook.

And they sang, and sang, and sang, and sang, with the rhythm and the power of one great, collective, beating heart.

❧

The natives seemed not at all inclined to leave. More came with others to be healed. And although Mary's spirit shared their joy, her weary body soon rebelled. She sank back into the carriage seat, hoping that Pastor Daniel would not forget the original purpose of their journey.

At least Emma hadn't. "I will speak to him, my dear."

She forced her way through the exuberant crowd, and when she had reached him, Pastor Daniel looked up. He nodded at Mary and smiled, then raised his hands, drawing the crowd to silence.

He was about to dismiss the service.

He wouldn't baptize her in front of all these people—not in her condition—surely not. Looking like an albino hippopotamus.

But he had a grander plan in mind.

No sooner had he announced that there was to be a baptism service, and it was translated by the interpreter, than the natives made a beeline for the river, splashing into the shallows in such numbers that Mary swore to Emma she could see the waters rise along its banks.

And among them, Kweela.

Inspired by the miracles, she, too, had jumped into the baptismal revelry.

Emma looked at Mary, and she at Emma, and together they burst into a joyous laughter that could not immediately be stemmed.

"My husband is not one to miss an opportunity," Emma declared, once she'd caught her breath.

And after all, wasn't that his calling? To bring the heathen to the Lord?

Finally, it was Mary's turn.

Emma helped her down the slope, with Nandi, Kweela, and Jalamba her spiritual support. Her little family gathered close as Pastor Daniel reached out, his hand strong and steady as he guided her through the chill water toward him.

Then it was only his dear face she saw and his deep, gentle voice she heard as he said, "Mary McKenzie, do you believe that Jesus Christ is the Son of the Living God?"

"I do," she whispered.

"Then I baptize you in the name of the Father, and the Son, and the Holy Spirit."

And down she went into the water, dead and buried, to be resurrected to her new life as a member of this glorious family of God.

As Pastor Daniel lifted her up, a resounding cheer rose from the crowd.

Laughing for joy, she stretched her arms to the heavens.

And then she saw him. A man on horseback at the edge of the crowd.

Colin.

She just stood there, unable to pull her eyes away. His gaze locked with hers, willing her to him.

She'd been baptized at the river like her Lord Jesus, and now, before she'd even left the water, her greatest temptation was upon her.

twelve

As Colin stared down at Mary from astride his stallion, he felt his pulse fuse with the ceaseless, exotic beat of the natives' upraised voices. He couldn't believe it. He'd been in the bush for months, and when he'd finally ventured back, the first white woman he laid his weary eyes on was Mary. And from the way his heart was pounding, he might as well have spared himself the trouble of leaving in the first place.

Surrounded by the press of statuesque, ebony-skinned Zulus, Mary's small, delicate frame, albeit bountiful with child, looked fragile and vulnerable. Glints of sunlight, brighter than the refractions off the Hope diamond, sparkled in the drops of water clinging to the wild waves of her wet hair and the lashes of her astonished brown eyes. And the chaste white shift, molded to her body, struck Colin as so provocative, it nearly drove him mad not to leap from his horse and sweep her into his arms.

Well, he guessed that answered the question.

Six months he'd been gone, and it was as if he'd never left. The woman couldn't be unhinged from his thoughts. Or his heart.

And, unless Ed McKenzie had been found since Colin had received his last report from Deputy Magistrate Scott, Mary was still without a husband. Something had to be done. After all this time, an annulment might be a real possibility, he thought hopefully.

Gathering up the hem of her dripping garment, Mary cast a despairing look back in Colin's direction, as with Kweela and Nandi's help, she hastened to the carriage.

Colin wheeled his horse and trotted back to his men, flanked on a crest overlooking the river. Putting Sergeant Bartlett in charge, he ordered them to proceed ahead to Johannesburg. He would follow in due course.

Among the dark-skinned natives, Daniel's pale face was more conspicuous than the moon in a night sky. Colin caught his eye and saluted. Dismounting, he tied his horse to the branch of a Mapeni tree and wove his way through the throng.

Daniel met him halfway up the slope. Wet from hips down, he extended a chilled hand and a warm greeting. "Glad you're back, old friend. Those few letters you sent haven't nearly compensated for the loss of your good company."

Colin laughed. "Doesn't look to me like you're lacking for companionship."

"God has done great things here today, Colin—"

A young native woman broke from the crowd, prostrating herself before Daniel, and began kissing his bare feet.

Daniel reached down and helped her rise. Shaking his head, he pointed to himself, then lifted his gaze and his arms to the sky.

The young woman's face seemed to light up with understanding. As she bowed and backed into the crowd, a tall, bearded Kaffir in a leopard skin tunic stepped forward.

His voice was deep and mellifluous, and he spoke with a cultivated British accent. "I will explain to the woman, Umfundici. I will make her understand that the healing of her child came from the Great Invisible God. But it is hard to explain to my people when they witness your magic."

"Not *my* magic," Daniel corrected. "God's miracles."

It seemed Daniel had been up to much more than merely one of his river baptisms.

Apparently sensing Colin's skepticism, the man turned and said sternly, "This day, people have been made well here. Even a lad with a cursed leg."

Colin nodded, struggling to maintain a composed expression. How easy it was for these simple folk to be duped. He saw it in the mines. He saw it here. Not that Daniel would do such a thing intentionally. But the natives were so gullible, so anxious to be convinced, that Colin suspected they conjured up ills just to have them cured. The miracles of Daniel's God were as authentic to them as their witch doctors' sorcery.

He glanced at Daniel and was struck by the sincerity and conviction burning in his friend's eyes.

To Daniel, his God was no sorcerer.

It was hard to believe that such a brilliant man could be so metaphysically seduced.

ช.

As the last Zulu stragglers disappeared over the crest of the hill and their singing faded into the distance, Mary reappeared with Emma. Colin struggled for calm. He must not give himself away to the Bryants. To covet a married woman was a grave sin to these fine Christian people—even to Colin, himself.

He tried not to stare at her, but he couldn't help himself. The true miracle here today was how this sweet girl could look so dainty and so fetching, when most women close to their time were heavy and awkward. She had changed into a loose-fitting dress and seemed to float toward him in a froth of blue as clear a color as the sky. Her hair was pulled into a bun at her crown, from which wisps of curls escaped, drifting softly about her glowing face.

The nearer they came, the more she lagged behind Emma, her shy gaze not quite reaching his.

Emma, however, was not reticent. "Colin, my dear boy, how wonderful. You're home at last. We've missed you." She gave him a hug and peck on each cheek.

"I've missed all of you, too," he replied, including Mary in his encompassing smile. "And our musicales. Native chants and jungle drums just don't quite do it."

"Now that you're back, we'll have to start up again," Daniel said.

Without Grace Ellen, I hope. Colin remembered that last evening they were all together.

"Unfortunately, we've lost Grace Ellen," Emma said.

There are such things as miracles, after all.

"She and her father are off to India."

To find other unsuspecting prey, no doubt. Colin felt almost giddy with relief.

"But we have met a charming couple who have recently moved here from Durban. Both musicians. She plays the. . ." Emma continued, but Colin was finding it very difficult to concentrate.

When he realized that she'd paused, he said, "You arrange the date, and I will most certainly be there," hoping she hadn't noticed his momentary lapse.

Emma smiled at Mary. "Not too soon, I think. Mary is expecting any day, now."

"It feels more like any minute."

Those were the first words Mary had spoken, and the mere sound of her soft, lilting voice made Colin's heart skip more than a beat.

"I don't suppose you've heard anything about Ed, or you would have written." Her large eyes were sad. "He doesn't even know he's going to be a father."

Emma squeezed her hand. "Have faith, little one. Remember what I said about God's promise. Everything will work out in the end."

Colin's jaw tightened. That fiction might be of comfort to Emma and Daniel, but they had no right to foist their fantasies on Mary. As far as Colin was concerned, the worst thing now would be if the cad did come back. Then Mary would be stuck with the shiftless no-account for the rest of her life.

Emma put her arm around Mary, shooting a warning look at the two men not to continue this conversation. "I think you've had enough excitement for one day, Mary dear. It's time we went home."

As she and Mary moved back to the carriage, Daniel took Colin aside. "You don't suppose her husband changed his name for some reason?" he asked quietly.

"Mary and I have already discussed that possibility."

"I mean before he and Mary were married. Maybe McKenzie isn't his real name."

"I suppose anything's possible." Colin glanced at Mary, glad enough for the excuse. "Even foul play."

They stood silent for a moment, neither wanting to expound on the possibility that Ed McKenzie might, in fact, be dead.

Daniel took a deep breath. "Well, good luck, old man. I hope you find him soon." He gave Colin's arm an encouraging squeeze as he turned.

Emma called, "You must come and have some of Nandi's good home cooking, Colin."

"Name the day," he answered, meeting Mary's gaze.

❧

As he reined up in front of the district headquarters in Johannesburg, Constable Peterson gave Colin a smart salute. "Welcome back, sir."

"Thank you, Peterson." Colin relinquished his horse to the officer and took the steps two at a time, acknowledging the greetings of his staff as he strode down the hall.

He'd been a fool to stay away so long, living in primitive conditions, eating less than palatable food. Scott, his second-in-command, was a competent man. He could have gone north and taken over the patrols once Colin set up the substations.

The last couple of months Colin had used even minor disturbances at the mines as an excuse for remaining in the Murchison District. . .to escape his own particular disturbances.

All the while, *this* was where his primary duty lay. It was time to admit he'd allowed personal feelings to interfere with his professional judgment.

He ran up the stairs and pushed open his office door.

Deputy Magistrate Scott's neat blond beard split with a smile as he put down the sheet of paper he was reading and marched across the room to shake his superior's hand. "Good to have you back, sir."

The two men looked eye to eye, but where Colin sported an enviable head of thick dark hair, Deputy Scott's was mostly on his chin. But his physique was as lean and hard as Colin's and they shared a sense of duty and commitment. He was a man who could be counted on, as Colin well knew.

"I've had tea prepared, sir. Unless you'd like something stronger."

"Tea will be fine."

Colin removed his cap and hung it on the hat rack, then moved to the window. He shoved his hands in his pockets and looked absently down onto the street, not yet ready to face the backlog of paperwork that had accumulated in his absence. Further evidence of his neglect.

He turned and accepted the cup of tea the deputy handed him. The first sip burned his tongue, and he sucked in air. "Hot. Just the way I like it."

Grinning at his colleague, he dropped into the chair behind his desk and gestured the other man to sit opposite. "Bring me up to date."

"The usual problems. Nothing exceptional. Except more of an influx of Kaffirs' wives and children."

Colin shook his head. "I'm not surprised."

"Some of the folks around here are starting to complain.

They don't like the shantytowns springing up on the outskirts."

"Instead, they should be outraged by how little the mines pay those poor men," Colin asserted. "Their families have to live somewhere."

"The folks claim crime has doubled." The deputy gave Colin a beleaguered look. "Not true, but try and convince them."

"Been giving you a hard time, have they?" Taking another swallow of tea, Colin smiled. "I'll tell you what. After you catch me up, how does a holiday sound?"

Scott looked painfully grateful. "My wife will take that as good news. She's seen very little of me since you've been gone. I must admit, now that I've had such an extended taste of your job, might I say, sir, you're welcome to it."

Colin pulled out his timepiece. "It's late. Why don't you go home. There are just a couple of things I want to check before I leave. We'll have a go at it tomorrow."

"Thank you, sir." Deputy Scott rose, tossed Colin a quick salute, and headed toward the door. "Oh. Bye the bye, sir—" He turned back. "Did you receive the message I sent about that fellow we've been searching for. . .McKenzie?"

"You've located McKenzie?" Colin lunged to his feet, rattling the half-empty cup and splashing its remaining contents into the saucer.

"No, not that. A United States marshal was in town last week asking about him. It appears McKenzie robbed some factory in New York City. The clever fellow led the authorities to think he'd gone to some northern territory. Alaska, I believe. Sent them on quite an ostrich chase. But they finally tracked him to a ship heading in our direction. The ship's captain remembered him in particular because he performed a wedding ceremony for McKenzie."

Colin stared into his empty cup.

There was no longer a shred of doubt.

Mary was married. And to a thief.

Absently he poured the splashed tea from the saucer back into the cup and handed it to Scott to dispose of.

He frowned. "I was just with Mrs. McKenzie and the Reverend and Mrs. Bryant. None of them mentioned anything about a visit from a United States marshal."

"Well, sir, I saw no reason to involve the poor woman. As we both know, she can't give the marshal any more information than we've already gotten from her. Was I wrong in shielding her, sir?"

"I would have done the same," Colin said, wondering just how many others besides himself had the urge to protect Mary. How many others, in his absence, had come to recognize her extraordinary qualities.

"On the other hand, sir, if she knew something about the theft—"

"I seriously doubt that. The woman is so honest, it would have been impossible for her to keep such a secret." Colin scratched his chin thoughtfully. "But if McKenzie's on the run, that makes it easier to see why he's been so hard to trace. He's changed his name, for sure. Maybe even dyed his hair." He looked up at the deputy. "Did the marshal say how much McKenzie stole?"

"No. But it must have been considerable. There's a reward for his capture of a thousand American dollars."

Colin's anger at Mary's husband spiked. There had been no reason for him to leave her penniless. No reason at all. . .

Unless he lost it all gambling aboard ship before he got here.

To Ryzzi Kryzika.

No wonder that little miscreant had been so evasive. If there was anything left to lift, Ryzzi certainly wouldn't have wanted the law mucking it up.

Well, Kryzika had a big surprise coming.

Colin was about to get some answers if he had to wring

them out of the runt's scrawny neck with his own bare hands.

He looked up at his deputy and actually smiled. "I think I know someone who is going to feel much more like talking than he did before."

"Because of the reward."

"That, too."

thirteen

Colin paced his office like a caged lion. It had been two days since he'd seen Mary at the river. Why hadn't he wangled an invitation for dinner at the Bryants' then?

Well, since he hadn't, and Emma had yet to be in touch, he'd have to plan another ploy.

He could always use the excuse of the U.S. marshal's visit. But he wouldn't.

Even his deputy knew better than to take the chance of upsetting a woman so close to her time.

He could stop by on his way to. . .wherever.

He glowered at the pile of papers on his desk. Six months' worth. He'd hardly made a dent. He seemed capable of little else than mooning about Mary.

At least he'd made some inroads into finding her husband. When Ryzzi Kryzika heard about the reward, the degenerate scoundrel was sure he could be "helpful." Colin was sure, too. For that kind of money the little ferret would turn on his own mother.

Colin could hardly wait. Once he'd apprehended McKenzie, he expected to exert *every* influence to convince the thief that a quick annulment would be in his best interests.

He raked his hand through his hair. Kryzika should have turned up something by now. It had been two days since their conversation.

Striding over to his office window, he leaned out and peered down the street toward Ryzzi Kryzika's "establishment." It was mid-afternoon, and as usual, that part of the street was relatively deserted. Ryzzi's "employees" were still asleep, and their customers didn't come out until after dark.

If he didn't hear from the little runt soon, he might just be forced to send a squad down at midnight to interrupt commerce.

Suddenly, something sparkled on a rise above the city. . . reflecting the sun. Henry's telescope? Colin chuckled, speculating where it was directed today.

For the first time, he felt a twinge of envy—not for Henry's wealth, but for the stability of his life and the love of his family. Loneliness surged through Colin. He wondered if those gifts would ever be his.

Just as he was about to pull in his head, he saw Daniel riding at a fast clip from the opposite direction. His friend had every appearance of a man on a mission. On his way to headquarters to see Colin?

For Mary.

Maybe she'd gotten wind of the U.S. marshal.

Burning with curiosity and concern, Colin hurried out of his office and down the stairs to greet his friend. He reached the street just as Daniel galloped by.

"Daniel," he shouted, running after him.

Daniel didn't stop, but reined his steed to a slower gait, allowing Colin to catch up. "Sorry. Can't talk. I'm after the doctor."

"Mary?"

Daniel nodded, visibly concerned.

"I'll fetch the doctor. You're needed at home." Colin swung around to a deputy loitering on the steps. "Saddle my horse!"

2a

Daniel's house had never seemed so far out of town, nor Dr. Lukin so slow—not even that sad night Colin had brought him for Emma.

Turning in his saddle, Colin shouted at the lagging buggy.

"Isn't it commonplace for a woman to have problems birthing her first child?"

The doctor stretched toward him, cupping his hand behind his ear. "What's that?"

"Problems," Colin shouted louder. "Don't some women have trouble with their first?"

The doctor nodded. "Some do." And he continued at the same ponderous clip.

"This is Mrs. McKenzie's first, you know," Colin shouted. "Maybe we should go a little faster."

"She's a strong, healthy girl. I wouldn't worry yet," the doctor called back, not increasing his speed by so much as a blink.

Yet?

Was the doctor crazy?

If not yet, when?

Colin was beside himself.

"Just the normal problems," the doctor called out.

"Problems? What problems?"

The fellow was so cavalier about it all. Colin could have strangled him. Didn't he understand how fragile Mary was?

He suddenly realized that the man was not only casual, but he was coming to a halt.

Had he not been the doctor, Colin would have throttled him on the spot. "Why are you stopping?" he roared.

Dr. Lukin gave him an indulgent smile. "We're here."

"Oh."

Colin pulled up his horse and hit the ground before the animal had completely stopped. Slipping the reins through the hitching ring, he hurried to help the doctor down from his buggy, then, carrying the man's medical bag, hustled him through the gate and up the walk. Not bothering to knock, he pushed open the front door, propelling the doctor before him.

Daniel strode down the hall toward them. "She's in here,"

he said, indicating Mary's door just past the parlor.

It occurred to Colin how strange his excessive concern must appear to Daniel, who had seen Mary with him only under the most circumspect of circumstances. He cleared his throat. "If I'm in the way, I'll go."

"Of course not." Daniel took his arm. "Let's see if Nandi has a pot of tea brewing. She usually does."

As they sat down at the kitchen table, a muffled cry came from down the hall.

"Mary—" Colin began to rise.

Daniel drew him back into the chair. "I fear you and I are of little use to her right now. The best thing we can do is pray."

"Why bother?" Colin, whose nerves were tighter than the strings on his violin, yanked away his arm. "It didn't help when your baby—" The words froze on his lips. "I'm sorry," he said roughly. Daniel was too good a man to hurt, no matter how blind and misguided he was with his platitudes and prayers.

Colin stared down at his clenched fists.

"I'm sorry," he repeated. Breathing a deep, despondent sigh, he looked up into Daniel's contemplative gaze.

Quietly, Daniel said, "I can't tell you why one baby dies and another is spared. But I do accept that our Heavenly Father loves Emma and me very much and, if we trust and believe in God's promise, good will come, even out of our baby's death."

"If it gives you comfort, so be it."

Daniel shook his head. "You're a hard sell, Colin." He shrugged. "Faith isn't something you can prove. It's. . .well, as the Bible says, it's the substance of things hoped for, the evidence of things not seen."

He contemplated his friend for a moment. "I'm going to confide in you." Pouring two cups of tea, he pushed one toward Colin. "It may not have appeared so on the surface, but since we came to South Africa, Emma and I had begun to lose touch. Both of us so busy. Me preaching, running the mission, and then being gone weeks at a time. Emma was wonderful, holding down the fort, keeping up with her women's Bible studies, helping the needy, playing the piano for the choir. It seemed our tasks were never done. Even *we* were too busy to notice."

He gazed down into his cup. "But underneath, we'd lost track of each other. Something was missing that we'd once had. And then our child died, and we were forced to look at ourselves and our relationship. Our loss brought us close again. Closer than we've ever been or even dreamed of being. Now, as the Bible says, we are as one. And that's the way we intend to remain. Always. So you see, Colin, that baby, however briefly on this earth, was a blessing."

If any face could be transformed by the Spirit of God—*if* there was such a thing—it would surely be Daniel's.

A long, silent minute passed before Colin said, "I envy you your faith. I, too, once believed, but. . ." His voice faded.

Daniel leaned forward, dropping his hand on Colin's arm, resting on the table, and looked into his eyes. "I'm convinced that spark of Christ is still in you, my friend. I pray that it will flame again, stronger than ever."

"Were it that easy," Colin muttered, averting his gaze.

At that instant, they heard Mary cry out, followed at once by the lusty wail of a baby.

Both men sprang to their feet.

It seemed an eternity that they waited, but it was only moments before Nandi rushed down the hall. "It is a girl!"

"Mary. How is Mary?" Colin cried.

"She is fine. The baby is fine. Mr. Colin, you got the doctor here just in time."

Colin had to see for himself.

Weak, but utterly grateful for a swift, if painful, delivery, Mary sat on the edge of the bed as Kweela helped her change into a clean gown.

Across the room, the doctor returned his instruments to his bag. But Mary's gaze was on her baby. She watched with wonderment as Emma cleaned and dressed the wee infant in the little gown that Mary had so lovingly embroidered. She could hardly believe that this squalling little bundle was actually her own dear baby girl.

Suddenly, the door burst open.

"Where is she? Is she all right?"

Colin! When did he get here? How?

"We're not quite ready for visitors yet," the doctor said.

Tugging down her gown, Mary peeked around Kweela and met Colin's eyes.

"Ah. . .yes. . .er, I'll wait outside," he mumbled, looking flustered, but hugely relieved.

As the door closed behind him, Kweela and the doctor exploded with laughter.

Nandi bustled into the room with fresh towels. "That Mr. Colin acts as nervous as if he is the papa."

"For someone who has not bothered to check for six months, he seems mightily concerned." Kweela picked up the large bowl of water from the nightstand. "Now that you are in bed, Missy, I will tell him to come in."

"I doubt you can get rid of him until you do." The doctor snapped his bag shut and followed Kweela and Nandi out the door.

Mary glanced up and caught Emma's eye. It lasted no longer than a heartbeat, but in that brief moment, she saw that Emma had perceived her feelings for Colin.

Emma tucked the blanket-wrapped baby into Mary's arms and smiled. "See how the little one stops crying when she's next to her mommy? She knows where she belongs."

Mary touched the incredibly downy hair, soft and shining as cornsilk in the sun.

"Dear heart," Emma said, "what a gift you have given us."

As Emma reached out and touched Mary's cheek, her expression of love filled Mary's heart to overflowing.

And then an ugly thought crept in.

Mary was glad, *glad* that it was Mrs. Emma, not Ed, with whom she'd shared this moment.

As Emma left the room, Colin entered. He stepped just inside the door, closing it behind him. He came no farther, but stood there, hesitant, silent, his eyes dark with emotion as his gaze traveled from Mary to the baby and back.

Mary could hardly breathe.

He cleared his throat. "All is well? With both of you?"

He loved her. And he loved her baby. She saw it in the way he looked at her, in every gesture he made. She heard it in the gentle timbre of his voice when he spoke to her. How could she not respond to such depth of feeling? "Yes—I mean, I think all is well." She offered him a tremulous smile and shifted her gaze to the baby. "I haven't counted all her fingers and toes yet, to see if she has the right number."

"Let me help."

What was the harm if just for this little time she pretended that he, not Ed, was her husband? That it was right for him to sit beside her as he was doing now.

He was so close. Only inches away. She could almost feel his breath on her wrist as she unwrapped the baby.

"You count the fingers." He lifted a wee foot in his large tanned hand. "I'll take the toes. Oh, but they are such tiny things."

As Mary heard the wonder in his voice and watched his tenderness, there was a poignancy in her joy. She dragged her gaze away.

Intent on her own endeavor, she picked up the little hand and held it in hers, caressing the velvet skin with her thumb. She marveled at its symmetry and perfection and wondered how anyone, looking at the miracle of a newborn baby, could doubt God's existence.

"I counted ten," Colin murmured. "How about you?"

"Me, too," she said, lifting her eyes to meet his.

"Good." His gaze lingered on her face, and his smile softened, then he reached down and touched the baby's soft, fine hair just as she'd done. "So silky." He examined the little face. "I think she has your eyes."

"My eyes are brown."

"I know," he said softly.

"Hers are blue, but dark blue. Perhaps they'll change."

"We'll just have to wait and see."

Oh, Colin, don't do this to me. Don't pretend we have a future together. Now is all there is.

"I predict she'll be a beauty like her mother."

Mary knew she should put a stop to this.

She shouldn't be listening to his loving words. She shouldn't *ache* to hear them.

"Have I—" He hesitated. "I hope I haven't overstepped the bounds."

"No." Unthinking, she touched his hand, and as quickly, pulled away. "Something just came to mind. It wasn't important."

But it was. Vitally.

"Have you picked a name for her yet?" he asked, looking relieved.

"I think I might name her Kathleen, after my mother. She died when I was twelve."

He touched the soft little blanket that Mary had wrapped again around the baby. "If she were mine, that's what I would want to do."

"Your mother died, too?"

"When I was a small boy."

"What was her name?"

"Elsa. Elsa VanRensburg was her maiden name."

"Isn't that Dutch?"

Colin nodded. "She was a wonderful mother. And a wonderful woman. Unfortunately, my father's family never accepted her."

His sad, distracted gaze tore at Mary's heart. She'd been in South Africa long enough to understand the English settlers' prejudice against the Dutch Boers. No wonder Colin was more tolerant than his peers of the less fortunate.

Mary's hand gravitated to his again. Softly, she said, "It must have been very hard for her."

"It was." Slowly, gently, as if not to frighten her, he turned his hand until it enfolded hers.

And her gaze was captured in the mesmerizing journey of his, following the line of her cheek, her lashes, the tip of her nose. . .her mouth.

Her breath suspended.

"Mary, dear." Emma was at the door.

Mary snatched back her hand.

Too late.

Emma glanced from her to Colin. "I think you need to rest now, dear."

Reluctantly, he rose and looked down, his lingering gaze palpable as a kiss.

Mary watched him go. She pulled the sleeping infant closer, leaned over, and touched its downy-soft head with her lips. Looking up, she met Emma's searching gaze.

Suddenly the guilt and fear and tears could not be stemmed. "Oh, Mrs. Emma," she sobbed. "I know it's a sin to love him so much. But I can't help myself, he's so good and kind and caring."

Emma dropped down onto the edge of the bed and wrapped

her arms around Mary and the baby. "I know, I know," she crooned, swaying with them, holding them close.

Mary felt like a baby herself, so vulnerable and small. "What am I to do? I'm a new Christian, and I'm so weak and the temptation is so strong."

Emma leaned back and looked into her eyes. Deep into her soul. "Don't be afraid, Mary. You must pray for strength. First Corinthians in the Bible promises that God will not let you be tempted beyond your strength."

"I will pray, Mrs. Emma. I will."

But would she be able to really mean the words?

fourteen

Colin tilted the bill of his cap lower to keep out the glare of the afternoon sun. From beneath the brim he studied Gordie Poole. The foul-smelling drunk swayed, nervously twisting his beat-up hat as he watched the two Kaffirs throw out shovels full of dirt from a hole—the spot where Gordie claimed Ed McKenzie was buried.

There were two things Colin was pretty sure of. First, that they'd find a body—whether or not it was McKenzie remained to be seen; and second, that Gordie knew more than he was telling.

This was one case where Colin was having a hard time keeping a professional detachment. If ever he'd wanted to find a man dead, God help him, it was now.

The irony was, Mary had been baptized just a few yards away. If this proved to be McKenzie, she might very well have stepped on her husband's grave.

No better than the blackguard deserved.

"There is something," one of the diggers yelled.

Pulse racing, Colin stepped closer to the edge and peered down.

With their callused hands, the two men threw out clods and brushed aside the dirt until a leg was exposed, then a torso, and finally, the entire decaying corpse.

Deputy Scott leaned over the pit. "I'd say he was about five-foot-nine or ten. What do you think?"

Colin grunted, his eyes on the tattered green shirt clinging to the last shreds of putrefied flesh. A tuft of wiry red hair sprang from above the deteriorated face.

One of the Kaffirs surreptitiously slid something into his pants pocket.

"I say, what do you have there?" Colin demanded.

Reluctantly, the guilty fellow dropped it into Colin's palm. A coin. A Spanish doubloon—like the one Mary had described. If the red hair hadn't been the clincher, the coin was.

"It looks like for once Gordie is telling the truth," the deputy murmured.

"I told ya," the drunk whined. "Now I'll be gettin' my reward."

It was McKenzie, all right, and if Gordie Poole was accurate, he'd been dead since last summer. The sucker probably never reached the outskirts of Johannesburg before he was murdered.

After all these months of looking. No wonder there'd been no trace of him.

Mary was a widow, had been all along. And Colin had a pretty good idea who had made her one.

He didn't know whether he wanted to give Kryzika a medal or a hangman's noose.

&

Mary sat at the kitchen table wrapped in a plum silk dressing gown that had once been Emma's. As she sipped her tea, she watched Emma and Nandi giving the babe a bath. Emma hummed along as Nandi sang a soothing lullaby in her native tongue.

Mary's heart was full. *I have so many blessings*, she thought. She *would not* stray again from God's precepts by dwelling on Colin. Now, with little Kathy to consider, there was too much at stake. She must lead an exemplary life, if for no other reason than to be a good example for her child.

Emma held up the baby, diapered and dressed in a new gown.

"I think pink is her color," Nandi said, chucking the baby

under her chin. "Don't you, Missy Mary?" She looked at Mary, then past her.

Mary turned.

Colin stood just inside the back door, but filled the kitchen with his presence.

Oh Father, give me strength.

He was in his military tunic and high-booted jodhpurs, holding his cap in his hand.

As he greeted the others, his eyes only grazed Mary. She sensed a remoteness in his behavior that seemed out of character. Clearly, something was bothering him.

"What do you think of our little Kathy?" Emma asked, holding the baby up.

"Dare I *not* say she's beautiful?" He smiled. "But anything else would be a lie." He touched one of the baby's tiny feet peeking out from under the gown. "And ten toes," he said softly.

Mary stared down into her cup. That was far from remote.

When she looked up, he was standing in front of her. "Mary, will you join me on the verandah. I have some official business to discuss."

"Of course." She shot a guilty glance at Emma.

Easing herself up, Mary felt Colin's hand at her elbow and sensed Emma and Nandi's eyes as he helped her rise. He supported her gently as they moved down the hall toward the French doors off the dining room.

"Do you want some tea, Mr. Colin?" Nandi called.

"No, thank you, Nandi."

Depositing Mary in one of the rattan chairs, he pulled another close and sat down, tossing his cap on the table.

"Is it too cool for you out here? Would you rather go back inside?"

She shook her head, concentrating on the flapped pocket of his tunic.

He took her hand.

Startled, she raised her eyes and was struck by his concerned expression.

"The mystery of your husband is over, Mary."

"You found Ed?"

Oh, no, she wanted to scream.

"His body," Colin said quietly.

"His body?" Had she heard correctly.

"I'm afraid, Mary, your husband met with foul play."

A chill ran through her. "Ed is dead?"

Colin nodded.

Even in her most embittered moments, when she never cared if she saw Ed again, she didn't wish him dead. Maybe once or twice it had occurred to her that he might be, and the thought hadn't saddened her as it should.

But that didn't mean she wished it.

"How? When?" She tried to withdraw her hands, but Colin held fast.

"We think he's been dead since the day he left for the northern gold fields. He scarcely got past the city limits."

Why wasn't she crying? She almost felt as if they were discussing a stranger. She glanced toward the kitchen. "Then I guess he didn't *actually* abandon us."

Colin shifted in his chair. His expression told her he didn't agree, but at least he didn't say so. "As much as I hate to tell you, I think you'd better hear it all," he said.

"There's more?"

"A United States marshal came by headquarters a couple of weeks ago, looking for an Ed McKenzie. Wanted for robbing a dress factory in New York. There was a sizable reward posted for his apprehension."

Ed? A thief?

Mary couldn't believe it. Her agitated gaze whirled around the verandah. She wouldn't believe it. Ed was hardly the ideal husband. But a thief?

But the more she thought about it, the more things fell into place—his eagerness to change their destination when he discovered the ship for South Africa left seven hours before the one for Alaska, and how he had all that money to gamble every night in the boiler room.

"Mary." Colin was squeezing her hand to get her attention. "There's more. I've arrested Ryzzi Kryzika, along with a couple of his cohorts, for the murder."

"Well, at least that doesn't surprise me. That man is capable of anything." She shook her head. "Poor Ed."

"Kryzika would have gotten away with it. But his greed got the best of him. Bilking your husband and murdering him wasn't enough. He couldn't resist the reward for locating him. But to get it, he had to produce the body. I won't go into the details, but, rest assured, he will be punished."

"Ed a thief and Ryzzi Kryzika a murderer," Mary murmured. "I came to South Africa in the company of very unsavory men."

Then a terrible thought occurred to her. "What does this mean for my baby, my little Kathleen? My sweet, innocent little girl? Why, she'll grow up with the stigma of a thief for a father. Who was *murdered*. The rest of her life she'll be living with that scandal." Mary could take anything dealt her, she already had, but the thought that her dear child would suffer was more than she could bear. Until then, she hadn't cried, but now the tears spilled, washing down her cheeks in a bitter flow.

Colin brought out his handkerchief and handed it to her. It wasn't the first time. She remembered when Peterson had brought her to his office the day she was arrested. Colin was so good and kind then, so sensitive. Just as he was being now. She wiped her eyes and balled the damp handkerchief in her fist.

"It doesn't have to be that way, Mary." Colin lifted her chin.

"In fact, little Kathy need never know about her father. You can count on Deputy Scott to remain discreet. As for Peterson, he's the only one who might talk. . .and I need him in the north country." He gave her a small smile. "Immediately." He leaned close. . .much too close. "It seems to me, the best thing is for you to remarry as soon as possible. Then, neither you nor the baby need bear McKenzie's name. It makes sense. You need a husband, she needs a father."

Suddenly, Colin stood up, as if his own words had shocked him. He ran his hand through his hair.

"Yes," he mused, "I think marriage is the answer for you."

For me! "And who, pray tell, did you have in mind? The vegetable man?" She lifted her tear-streaked face and glared at him. She did have some pride, after all.

Colin looked astounded. "Why, Mary, I'd never expect you to marry *him*."

"Why not? He's very nice."

"His name is Dhimitrakopoulus. Mary Dhimitrako-poulus?" Colin shook his head. "You've become a very good speller, but that name might be too much of a challenge, even for you."

First he plans her future and then he ridicules her.

"Me, Mary. I want you to marry me." His voice softened and he dropped back into his chair, taking her hands into his. "I know I'm speaking too soon. But please think about it. I love you, and I'd do everything in my power to give you a good life."

She could not believe what she was hearing. She reached up and touched his cheek. "What did you say?"

He turned his face into her hand and kissed it. "I said, marry me. I love you. I tried hard to stay away from you, knowing you weren't free to return my love. Six months I stayed away, and then one look at you, and it was as if I'd never left."

"Oh, Colin. I know, I know. No matter how hard I tried, I couldn't help loving you, either."

It had happened so fast. One minute she was Ed's wife; the next, his widow. And now she was receiving a proposal of marriage from the man she so desperately loved.

She smiled up at him. "Emma was right. Things do work out for the best for those who love the Lord. God is so good."

Colin cleared his throat and glanced away. "I suppose," he mumbled.

Colin's wife.

Reality ripped through Mary like a bolt of lightning.

She took a ragged breath. "Oh, my beloved. You have been—you are—my sweet, sweet temptation. . .but. . .I cannot marry you."

Colin stiffened, his expression incredulous. "Why ever not?"

"I'm a Christian."

"What difference could that possibly make?"

"You are not."

"I see no problem with your going to church. A lot of my friends do. And if it will make you happy, I'll even escort you there myself."

How convincing he was. How easy it would be to say yes, when she loved him so desperately. Becoming Colin's wife had been an ephemeral dream. But faced with its reality, now that she was a Christian, she realized that he was no more accessible to her than when she was Ed's wife.

Through her wash of tears, she could see the hurt clouding his eyes. If only she could make him understand. She twisted his damp handkerchief between her fingers, searching for a way, knowing that no matter how she couched the words, their wound would be as deep.

"In these last months I've come to know how important it is to share my belief in God with those close to me." As she spoke, miraculously, her resolve strengthened—at least for that moment. "If I marry again, it must be to someone who loves God as much as he loves me. Someone who will want to live by His precepts and teach them to our children."

She felt as if she were thrusting a sword into his heart. And her own. "You're not that man, Colin."

Again, Colin came to his feet. Anger and hurt pride flinted his eyes. "I should never have brought you here. These people have filled you with fairy tales. They've stolen your senses." He swung away from her. "If you ever retrieve them, let me know."

fifteen

Colin leaped onto his horse. He dug his heels into the stallion's flanks, and it shot forward. Barely did he notice the landscape flying by or hear the horse's hooves pounding the dusty road, or the hollow clatter as they crossed the bridge. He was propelled by the volatile mix of anger, pride, and pain that churned within him. His eyes were blinded by the sight of Mary's sad face; his ears rang with her final words.

"You're not that man, Colin."

Who did she think she was that she could toy with him the way she had?

She even said she loved me.

Loved me. Ha!

What a fool he'd made of himself. He hadn't come intending to offer marriage. But she'd looked so forlorn, so lost when he'd told her about Ed. And there was no one to take care of her and the baby. He took pity on her. It was out of the goodness of his heart. Had he not been so convinced she loved him, he never would have considered asking her to marry him at such an unorthodox moment.

He confessed his love for her. And she him. And her eyes had told him more, so much more.

Then she rejected him!

Him, the district magistrate.

Was she holding out for better?

If so, her chances were slim to none. No other gentleman of education and good repute would offer himself to an ignorant little factory worker from America. Barely able to read or write. And who would take care of her when the Bryants were gone? Another ne'er-do-well like Ed McKenzie or Fourth Street Ryzzi?

If she thought she could come crawling back to Colin then, she had another think coming.

How could she treat him so cruelly? His dear, sweet Mary. His brave little Mary. His beautiful, kind Mary.

It was those people. Those Bryants. He'd been a fool to take her to those fanatics. All they did was fill her mind with nonsense about an amorphous God. A specter. Neither to be seen nor heard. Let alone proved.

Colin was a modern, sophisticated man, a hard-headed realist. A man of the twentieth century. His life's work was built on provable facts. He'd gone to Oxford, by heaven. He was no dimwit who fantasized about some ubiquitous phantom.

Nearing the center of town, he slowed his mount. He couldn't face going back to headquarters, not yet. He needed to sort things out. If only there was someone he could talk to.

Daniel.

Always the first person he thought of when he had a problem.

What a farce that was. Daniel was responsible for Mary's delusion.

If anything, he was more deluded than she.

And if he spoke to Henry, his old chum would just smirk and make some inane remark.

No, he'd have to go this one alone.

❧

"Colin was certainly in a hurry." Emma ventured as she walked out onto the verandah, carrying Baby Kathy in her arms.

Mary stared at her dumbly. How long had she been sitting here, frozen, numb?

"It's not like him to leave without saying good-bye—there you are, my little darling." Emma laid the infant in Mary's arms and dropped into the chair that Colin had vacated.

"Why, my dear, what is the matter?"

Mary hugged the baby against her breast. "Oh, Mrs. Emma, sometimes it's so hard to be a Christian."

Emma reached out and stroked Mary's arm. "Did Colin bring bad news?"

Mary nodded, rubbing her cheek against the sleeping baby's fine Titian curls. "They found Ed's body."

"Oh, my dear—"

"Murdered before he barely got out of town." Mary drew a sobbing breath. "Poor Ed."

"I'm so sorry. So very sorry."

"I also learned he was a wanted criminal. An unsavory character, Mrs. Emma, but I wouldn't have wished him dead."

"I know dear, I know." Emma pulled her chair closer, encircling the trembling girl in her embrace.

"It was that Ryzzi Kryzika that killed him," Mary murmured into Emma's shoulder. "If anybody would do such a thing, it was that evil man." Mary pulled away from Emma, her heart bleak. "It's not that I was all that shocked about Ed. It had been so long since anything had been heard of him, I'd begun to wonder at the possibility that maybe he was dead. But still, to hear the words. . ."

"So much trouble for such young shoulders to carry." Emma leaned back and lifted Mary's chin. "But now you understand that you need not bear the burden alone. Our Lord is here to sustain and support you."

"I know," Mary murmured, tears spilling down her cheeks. "I can't imagine what I would have done had I not had that assurance."

"And, my dearest, you can count on Daniel and me for as long as you need us." Emma stroked her arm again. "You know that."

"But there's more, Mrs. Emma." Mary lifted stricken eyes.

"Your brothers. Something's happened to your brothers?"

She shook her head. "It's Magistrate—it's Colin. He asked me to marry him."

"And you said?"

"I had to tell him no, because. . .because—"

"He's not a Christian."

Emma's words twisted Mary's heart.

Again the dear woman's arms locked around her and the baby in an embrace of love and protection. "No wonder he raced out of here as if he were on fire."

"It's so hard, Mrs. Emma. He's so good, so compassionate. And I've heard you talk about how he treats everyone with equal kindness and justice. Natives, the Dutch settlers—even me, when I first came to South Africa and had no one."

"He is, indeed, a good man," Emma agreed, "and a reason for much prayer. Daniel has not a better friend in Africa. And yet, there is always that separation, that gulf, between them."

Mary turned sorrowful eyes in the direction of town. "That one great gulf," she whispered, the tears beginning to flow again.

❧

It had been two weeks since Colin had seen Mary, given her the news about Ed. . .asked her to be his wife.

Been rejected.

For two weeks he'd done his job with brusque efficiency and little patience. His staff had been wise enough to give him a wide berth.

He could hardly blame them.

He'd felt no inclination to accept any social engagements, sparing his friends the burden of his disagreeable presence. Rather, he had sought the silence and solace of his books— and his own bleak thoughts.

Little comfort there.

The report of a minor skirmish at the Stratton Mine had just come in. And he was grateful. It gave him the excuse he needed to get out of town, now that his second-in-command was back from holiday.

But before he left, he felt obliged to visit Henry.

Much to his relief, Sylvia was nowhere in sight when the servant answered the door, and Colin managed to slip up the three flights to Henry's "playroom" without being observed.

After a hearty greeting, and "It's about time you showed up, old man," Henry said, "You're in luck. My little lady is having tea with the Carter twins. Had you been a moment sooner, no doubt she'd have dragged you along. Family just moved here from Durban—bring us some iced cider, Modjadji," he interjected to the servant who had followed Colin up. "New brand my brother-in-law shipped from the UK—with Grace Ellen gone—"

"So I heard." Even now, Colin's spirits rose a tad at the thought.

"Don't expect Sylvia to give up that easily, m'boy. She's checking out the Carter sisters as we speak. Say, what about the little wren? Hear she had her baby. Ever locate her husband?"

Much to Colin's relief, Henry didn't pause for a reply, but moved toward a large table in the middle of the room covered by an intricate landscape of city streets and buildings, mountains, trees, a running stream and waterwheel. He flicked a switch and a train moved out of the depot. "Did you ever see anything like it? All battery-operated. I've been working on it for weeks. It's for my son."

"So I see." Colin smiled.

"You won't be smiling when you have a boy of your own, old chap."

Henry's words rubbed salt into Colin's wounded heart. He looked toward the window, but found no comfort there, as his eyes fell on the telescope and he was reminded of the first day he'd caught sight of his sweet Mary.

"I wanted to see you before I headed north," he said.

"Again?"

"Labor problems at the Stratton Mine."

"Seems to me we've got as many problems in the mines around here—watch how the train takes the mountain—"

At that moment the servant came huffing up the stairs with iced glasses of cider, and Henry turned off the switch. The two men sat down in a couple of easy chairs on a small porch overhanging the garden.

Henry took a long draught and sighed. Leaning back, he crossed his legs. "What do you think of all the excitement?"

"You mean the body we dug up?" Colin asked tentatively, unwilling to give more information about the case than absolutely required.

Henry waved a dismissive hand. "Not that. Murder and mayhem are standard fare around here. I'm talking about Daniel's miracle. It's all over Johannesburg."

Colin lifted a censuring brow. "Come now, Henry."

Henry leaned forward. "I'm serious. You know Nyati, that Kaffir who delivers chickens? The one with the lame son he pulls around in the cart? It seems he was at Daniel's healing service a couple of weeks ago. Now, the boy's leg is as straight as an arrow. I'm surprised you didn't hear about it."

Colin shook his head. "You're as gullible as the natives. I thought you Anglicans had more sense."

"And you're as hard-headed as my marble bust of Caesar Augustus. But I don't blame you. I didn't accept it either, till I saw it for myself. One look at that restored leg made a believer out of me. And he's had other healing, too, I understand. Starting next Sunday, Sylvia and I are taking the children and going to Daniel's church."

"Come on, Henry," Colin scoffed, "you've been duped. It's got to be a different boy."

The good-natured man looked annoyed. "I'm not a simpleton, Colin. I've seen that lad since he was a tike. He has a large birthmark on his cheek and a withered—*had* a withered leg."

Was it possible? Colin's heart pounded. Henry had a tendency to exaggerate sometimes, but he was no liar. He studied his friend. The man was deadly serious. If it was a hoax, Henry was completely and honestly taken in.

And there was certainly no way Daniel would knowingly perpetrate a hoax. Mass hysteria. That's what it had to be. Colin had read of such things.

"Check it out yourself," Henry said.

Colin rose abruptly. "I think I will." Even as he strode out, he couldn't believe he was giving credence to the possibility.

"I didn't mean now," Henry said, lumbering to his feet and following Colin to the door.

But Colin was already halfway down the stairs.

❧

It took some doing, but Colin found Nyati's small poultry farm located at the end of a dirt track on the outskirts of town.

As he approached, he saw Nyati, a tall, scrawny Kaffir, his head shaded by a wide-brimmed straw hat, standing in a wire-fenced enclosure, tossing grain from a cotton sack to the frenetically pecking and squawking chickens. Spotting Colin, the man threw a large handful of feed into a corner and escaped out the gate opposite.

With a merchant's smile and handshake, he greeted his visitor.

At that moment, a lad came around the corner of a coop, lugging a fresh bag of seed. He had a birthmark on his cheek, red, in the shape of a ragged-edged *C*.

The birthmark of Nyati's son!

Colin's gaze shifted to the boy's leg.

His throat constricted.

The once twisted limb was, indeed, straight as an arrow. And as far as Colin could see, in shape and size, perfectly matched to the other.

"But how?"

"A miracle from the God of Umfundici—of Reverend Daniel." Nyati's black eyes blazed with the fire of his faith.

Colin could only stare at the boy, who by now had dragged the heavy bag across the yard. And he continued staring until the youth disappeared from view behind a shed.

And still Colin stared, as the carefully crafted structure of his disbelief crumbled and fell from him, dry and useless as the dust beneath his feet.

He could not remember mounting his horse, or where he rode, or for how long.

Thoughts tumbled over one another, disjointed and in disarray. He remembered the woman at the river kissing Daniel's feet and Daniel explaining to the tall, bearded native, "It is not my magic, it is God's miracle."

How Colin had scoffed at that.

And he remembered so much more.

He remembered the many debates he'd waged with Daniel those weeks on the road. Daniel's simple expression of faith as, together, they'd awaited the birth of Mary's baby. And he remembered his own rude reply. *If it gives you comfort.* As if only a fool could believe.

He, Colin, was the fool.

When he lifted his eyes, he found he had reined up in front of a whitewashed Dutch-styled structure, bathed in sunshine, surrounded by tended grass and shaded by oaks.

High above the double gothic doors, a simple wooden cross rose up.

Daniel's church.

How Colin had arrived there was a miracle in itself, for he had not consciously determined this destination. And yet he had no doubt that this was where he was meant to come.

Suddenly he became achingly aware of the beauty that surrounded him, the scent of the myrtle and bright-hued cannas skirting the mission, the warmth of the sun, the caress of a gentle breeze. As he dismounted, he heard the chirp of a bird nesting in the oak above him and bees buzzing in a nearby hive. His boots trod silently across the grass and clacked up the wooden steps.

It was cool in the narthex as he stood, gazing into the sanctuary.

The interior was polished oak; the floor, the walls, the pews angled toward the altar. Rectangles of light from the high windows along the eaves marched down the opposing side.

And rising above it all, the cross. The cross that symbolized the sacrificial death of Daniel's Lord Jesus.

Colin's step echoed as he walked down the middle aisle and slipped into a pew near the back.

The sanctuary was so silent. As he sat gazing up at that empty cross, he imagined he could hear his own heart beating, echoing inside his emptiness. He felt as if he were a vessel that had been drained, and there was nothing left to fill it.

If You're as real as they say You are, Jesus, show Yourself to me.

"Colin."

He looked up.

Daniel was standing beside him. And in his dear friend's face he saw reflected there what he so desperately sought. . . God's mercy, forgiveness, and love.

Tears clogged Colin's throat. "Tell me," he whispered hoarsely, "tell me everything I need to know."

sixteen

Mary buried her nose in the pink cabbage rose, drew a long, deep breath of the heady scent, and reluctantly added the blossom to the arrangement in the cut-glass vase. She'd already set the small table on the verandah with Emma's finest linens, the delicate, leaf-embossed Wedgewood, and etched sterling.

Emma did not believe in saving her best just for guests.

The English habit of tea was Mary's favorite time of day. She was glad the Bryants had adopted it and intended to do the same when she had a home of her own.

Absently, she plucked a flowering twig of jasmine from a twining patch and tucked it into her chestnut bun.

The length of the shadows angling across the lawn told her that Daniel was later than usual. And Emma, never one to while away a useless moment, had gone to the study to finish letters to her sisters until he arrived home.

A mottled brown-feathered fowl scuttled across a corner of the terrace, followed by a string of chicks.

Mary smiled. In a year's time her own little chick would be scurrying after her.

A year from now.

She'd just learned that the Bryants' mission in South Africa was not permanent. Next year, when their tour of duty was up, they could very well be sent to some other location, even to another country. Mary would be on her own.

She adjusted a rose in the bouquet.

Her need to earn money had taken on an urgency. Emma was certainly doing her part to help, touting Mary's skills as a seamstress to every lady she knew.

Mary smoothed the pleats of the pale yellow lawn dress she'd made just before the baby arrived. Still a little snug, but less so than a week ago.

If she managed her money very carefully, and with a little help from Ethan and Brody, she expected to have enough saved for her ticket to California by this time next year. Maybe even sooner.

The sooner the better.

She would miss the Bryants. Desperately. But she knew that her two active brothers, still in their teens, needed her there to introduce them to the good news of the Lord, to say nothing of some adult supervision. Who knew what those two were up to, off on their own?

But there was a more pressing reason she was so anxious to leave.

Colin.

The temptation to go to him, beg him to forgive her, to take her back, was always there, tugging at her resolve. No amount of praying had eased her longing for him. Putting half a world between them seemed like her safest choice.

Not that she ever saw him. But there was always that small glimmer of possibility. Perhaps catch a glimpse of him when she and Mrs. Emma went into town on their errands, or on their way to church, or. . .

She shook her head, determined to clear it of the hopeless musings that would sink her into that wretched melancholia that was always hovering at the edge of her thoughts.

With brisk determination she turned, but paused when she heard Daniel's approaching step on the gravel path.

But it was not Daniel.

It was Colin!

Mary sagged against the wicker chair as he stepped into the shade of the verandah. Her heart raced with such a frantic beat she feared it might burst from her breast.

Was it truly he? Or a cruel imagining?

Real or imagined, oh, he was so beautiful to her. . .his mantle of curling hair, catching blue lights in the black, his sculpted features and bronzed skin, his virile body made more so by the smart fit of his beige tunic and the highly polished boots.

The sight of him drew away the air she breathed. Her mouth went dry, her palms moist.

She stared at him, unable to utter a sound.

As if he were a thirsty man finding an oasis, Colin's dark eyes consumed her.

"Mary." His voice was low and hoarse with emotion. "Mary—" It grew in strength as he spoke. "The most amazing thing has happened."

He took a step forward. She, back.

He stood then, at ease. A smile began and broadened. Startling, wondrously beautiful. "A miraculous thing. As miraculous as. . .as. . .Nyati's son's withered leg becoming whole." His smile broke into a joyful grin. "Well, almost."

Again he took a step forward, and Mary retreated. Again he paused, waited, stalking the bird that really had no heart for flight.

"How does that hymn go? *I was lost*—me, the one with a compass always in his pocket. *But now I'm found. I was blind, but now I see*— Oh, Mary, I was deaf and dumb and arrogant. So arrogant I couldn't open my mind and heart to what was right in front of me."

No! Mary's hands flew to her flushed cheeks. *It can't be. He's just saying this to placate me. To trick me.* She lowered her gaze, blinded by his smile.

"Mary, look at me. Can't you see it?" he beseeched. "I don't know how to put it into words. My heart is so full."

Why would he pretend if it weren't so? Would he stoop so low to win her?

Not Colin. Never. He was too honest. Too proud.

"I believe in Him again, Mary. In His power and mercy. But I have so much to learn. Help me." He reached out his hand.

She looked at it—at him. "When? How?"

"Today, not more than an hour ago. It's as if I found Him and myself at the same time. You were so right. This is a joy that must be shared. . .especially with the one you love."

"Oh, my. Oh, dear." She reached for Colin and he pulled her to him. "My darling, my beloved," she sighed, melting into his arms.

She felt his lips, warm against her temple, the tip of her ear, the crest of her cheek. A thrill of excitement ran through her, and she clung to him as at last his mouth found hers and she felt its pressure, moist and moving, with a tenderness and yearning that echoed her own.

Breathless, Mary drew back, gazing up into his dear, beloved face. How could she have misread the truth in his eyes?

Oh ye of little faith. She had prayed to the Lord, yet not trusted His answer.

But now her own heart was open, and she saw it all, shining in Colin's countenance, bright as God's promise.

❧

Tilting her head, Mary studied her reflection in the full-length mirror as Kweela hooked the thirty tiny covered buttons that marched down the back of Mary's dress.

"You do not worry. I know Mr. Colin puts value on you, even though he brings not one cow—not even a goat," she muttered under her breath. The girl had tried to sound reassuring, but was having trouble hiding her disdain.

Mary struggled to suppress a smile as she adjusted the delicate tucks that made up the bodice of her ecru silk wedding gown. "That's not fair, Kweela, we just have different customs. It's true Magistrate Reed didn't give Pastor Daniel any cows for me, but he's spending a great deal of money on our honeymoon."

"What is a honeymoon?" Kweela asked suspiciously, adjusting the swagged backfolds of the soft fabric. Kweela had had her hand in the making of the exquisite garment, as had Emma. Even Nandi had offered an opinion. But the dress was Mary's design, and it was her fingers that had stitched the final seams and each tiny tuck.

"The first weeks after a wedding are called the honeymoon," Mary explained. "Couples who can afford to usually go on a trip. Just the two of them. But Colin is taking me *and* the baby to California to see my brothers—which will cost at least as much as a hundred cows. Maybe more."

Round-eyed, Kweela peeked over Mary's shoulder and met her reflected gaze. "That many?" Clearly, the young maiden, dressed in her own most colorful garments, was impressed. "Well, good."

Mary giggled. "Very good, indeed."

Over by the window, the baby mewed in her cradle, and Mary turned.

"Now, you do not move until I am done, Missy Mary. That young one can wait to be picked up." Kweela tucked a coronet of tiny fresh gardenias around the cascade of auburn curls drawn up at Mary's crown, and stood back to admire her handiwork. "You are a perfectly beauteous bride. Nobody can doubt that."

Mary smiled. "Thank you, Kweela. Perhaps you'll be next."

Looking down, Mary wondered if she'd forgotten anything. She touched Mrs. Emma's lace hankie embroidered with forget-me-nots that she'd tucked into her sleeve. Something borrowed *and* blue. And Baby Kathy certainly qualified for something new.

As for something old—she had folded four one-pound

notes into her luggage to give Colin later—an old debt. The amount he'd paid on her hotel bill the first day they met.

She was ready.

The sweet fragrance of the delicate gardenias wafted around her like the most expensive perfume as she gazed at her image in the mirror. What she saw was a young woman she wouldn't have recognized a year ago. And it was much more than the clothes she saw.

She saw a young woman with sparkling eyes, whose face shown bright with the joy of the Lord. A young woman who knew God's blessings and was grateful. It was not her own beauty that Mary saw, but the beauty of the Holy Spirit within her. And it filled the room.

"Missy Mary!" Nandi's voice and impatient fist hit the bedroom door. "Mr. Colin says if you do not come soon, he will think you ran out on him."

Kweela hollered back, "You tell Mr. Colin to hold his horses. She comes when she is ready." She turned to Mary. "It is not Mr. Colin anyway, it is that Nandi who is impatient. You just take your time." She strode toward the door. "I am going out there and set her straight."

As the door closed behind Kweela, Mary walked over to the window. She stood by the cradle, letting the sights and sounds of this beloved place wash over her for the last time as Mary McKenzie.

When she returned, it would be as Mary Reed.

Mrs. Colin Reed.

She sighed. This room had seen her many incarnations. Her baptism, the birth of her child, and now, her marriage.

She felt a moment's sadness, remembering how different this was from her first hasty wedding. How different the wedding. How different the man. But she never would have known the extent of Colin's goodness had she not first known Ed.

Perhaps that, too, was part of God's mercy. Ed had been her choice, not God's, but He had seen that good came from it. *The Lord works in mysterious ways, his wonders to perform.*

And it was a wonder, how she and Colin found each other.

How they'd both found Jesus.

She looked down at her beautiful baby girl, Ed's legacy that he would never know. And soon to be, in every way, Colin's child. She smoothed the batiste gown, as delicate and lovely as Mary's hands could fashion, then picked up her baby.

Kathleen Elsa.

The Elsa, for Colin's mother—Mary's gift that she was saving to tell him when they were alone.

She brushed her lips across the infant's soft cheek. "You are my flower, dear one, my bouquet."

As Mary walked down the hall, she heard the murmur of voices in the parlor where the wedding would take place. With the exception of Ethan and Brody, all those she loved most would be there. Jalamba, in his Sunday black suit and starched collar. Nandi would be in her favorite native costume, the orange-dyed fabric slashed with a symmetrical black-and-white tribal design. And Kweela, wearing the bright colors that signified a maiden's eligibility.

Emma at the upright. Mrs. Emma, her beloved sister in Christ.

And Pastor Daniel in his dark robes, his Bible in hand. Beside him, Colin.

Colin.

Where she'd felt so calm and sure just moments ago, Mary was suddenly overwhelmed with emotion. Her footsteps slowed. Before reaching the parlor archway, she paused. She pictured each kind, gentle face turned in her direction—even Nandi's.

Her eyes misted and her throat clogged with tears.

Had the baby not let out a small cry, who knows how long she would have remained.

She stepped through the curving arch, and it was as she'd imagined. There her loved ones were, the light of God's blessing.

And Colin, tall and magnificent, whose eyes alone she sought. Waiting for her.

As he would be always.

Now and forever.

epilogue

Overseer Daniel Bryant with his wife, Elder Emma Dempsey Bryant, started a mission in South Africa in 1904. They were greatly beloved and remained for several years, returning to America for the birth of their second child, a son.

The natives called Bryant the modern Moses, and when he returned briefly several years later, they lined the road for three miles to welcome him.

The mission is still active today.

A Letter To Our Readers

Dear Reader:

In order that we might better contribute to your reading enjoyment, we would appreciate your taking a few minutes to respond to the following questions. We welcome your comments and read each form and letter we receive. When completed, please return to the following:

Rebecca Germany, Fiction Editor
Heartsong Presents
PO Box 719
Uhrichsville, Ohio 44683

1. Did you enjoy reading *Out of the Darkness*?
   ❑ Very much. I would like to see more books
   by this author!
   ❑ Moderately
   I would have enjoyed it more if _____

   _____

   _____

2. Are you a member of **Heartsong Presents**? Yes ❑ No ❑
   If no, where did you purchase this book? _____

   _____

3. How would you rate, on a scale from 1 (poor) to 5 (superior), the cover design? _____

4. On a scale from 1 (poor) to 10 (superior), please rate the following elements.

   _____ Heroine   _____ Plot

   _____ Hero   _____ Inspirational theme

   _____ Setting   _____ Secondary characters

5. These characters were special because_____

_____

_____

6. How has this book inspired your life?_____

_____

_____

7. What settings would you like to see covered in future
   Heartsong Presents books?_____

_____

_____

8. What are some inspirational themes you would like to see
   treated in future books?_____

_____

_____

9. Would you be interested in reading other **Heartsong
   Presents** titles?   Yes ❏   No ❏

10. Please check your age range:
    ❏ Under 18   ❏ 18-24   ❏ 25-34
    ❏ 35-45   ❏ 46-55   ❏ Over 55

11. How many hours per week do you read?_____

Name _____

Occupation _____

Address _____

City _____ State _____ Zip _____

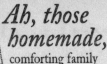

Ah, those homemade,

comforting family dinners around the table. But who has time to make them between carpooling and softball games?

Don't let your busy schedule deter you. This collection of delectable recipes—from the readers and authors of inspirational romances—has been gathered from all over the United States, and even from Greece and Australia.

There are tried and true recipes for every occasion—Crock-Pot meals for busy days, fast desserts for church dinners, rave snacks for after school, holiday gifts for those picky relatives, and much, much more. Over 700 recipes await you! Bring back the joy of treasured moments over good food with the ones you love. So, dust off the china and treat your loved ones (and yourself) to some delicious home cooking.

The Heart's Delight *cookbook has what every family needs—cooking from the heart.*

400 pages, Paperbound, 8" x 5 ³⁄₁₆"

Please send me _____ copies of *Heart's Delight*. I am enclosing $4.97 each. (Please add $1.00 to cover postage and handling per order. OH add 6% tax.)

Send check or money order, no cash or C.O.D.s please.

Name_____

Address_____

City, State, Zip_____

To place a credit card order, call 1-800-847-8270.
Send to: Heartsong Presents Reader Service
PO Box 719, Uhrichsville, OH 44683

·········· Presents ··········

Great Inspirational Romance at a Great Price!

Heartsong Presents books are inspirational romances in contemporary and historical settings, designed to give you an enjoyable, spirit-lifting reading experience. You can choose wonderfully written titles from some of today's best authors like Peggy Darty, Sally Laity, Tracie Peterson, Colleen L. Reece, Lauraine Snelling, and many others.

When ordering quantities less than twelve, above titles are $2.95 each.
Not all titles may be available at time of order.

Hearts♥ng Presents
Love Stories Are Rated G!

That's for godly, gratifying, and of course, great! If you love a thrilling love story, but don't appreciate the sordidness of some popular paperback romances, **Heartsong Presents** is for you. In fact, **Heartsong Presents** is the *only inspirational romance book club*, the only one featuring love stories where Christian faith is the primary ingredient in a marriage relationship.

Sign up today to receive your first set of four, never before published Christian romances. Send no money now; you will receive a bill with the first shipment. You may cancel at any time without obligation, and if you aren't completely satisfied with any selection, you may return the books for an immediate refund!

Imagine. . .four new romances every four weeks—two historical, two contemporary—with men and women like you who long to meet the one God has chosen as the love of their lives. . .all for the low price of $9.97 postpaid.

To join, simply complete the coupon below and mail to the address provided. **Heartsong Presents** romances are rated G for another reason: They'll arrive *Godspeed!*